Dash & Laila

Is there a stronger adversary than Fate?

Brad Chisholm

Black Rose Writing | Texas

ISBN: 978-1-68433-583-1
PUBLISHED BY BLACK ROSE WRITING
www.blackrosewriting.com

Printed in the United States of America
Suggested Retail Price (SRP) $18.95

Dash & Laila is printed in Chaparral Pro

*As a planet-friendly publisher, Black Rose Writing does its best to eliminate
unnecessary waste to reduce paper usage and energy costs, while never compromising
the reading experience. As a result, the final word count vs. page count may not meet
common expectations.

For Claire & Cole For Always.

With thanks to Reagan Rothe and Linda Langton.

Dash & Laila

Dasht & Laila

Chapter 1

You don't shoot a girl's ear off without consequences. Especially when the ear belongs to Laila, the hottest girl in the universe. While that hasn't actually happened yet, I am admittedly shaking at the prospect.

She came to detention today not wearing a bra. How is anyone supposed to study in these conditions? It's torture, if you think about it. In a contest between Mr. Mulch's English Lit lecture and Laila? Sorry, it isn't even close.

Not even girls speak to Laila, like ever. She is just too much. Too lithe with coppery skin and green eyes. Even the hottest girls are intimidated. Today she is wearing black ear pods, which is so unfair because Mr. Mulch can't see them under luxuriant dark hair which waterfalls down her back, tied into some exotic silk scarf.

Worse is her scent, which isn't from some commercial. It has weight, it is profound, it makes the little hairs on the back of my neck stand up.

Detention. A Saturday. It is cruel, and whatever Laila did to deserve this I have no idea. It's not like we talk much. Maybe that's just as well. Half a dozen sinners. Not bad enough to call the parents, or the cops, but enough to make us suffer.

In class Mr. Mulch was still droning on about some dead writer from some place where you can swim in the Mediterranean just like whenever. Maybe Mr. Mulch was making it sound worse than it was, which was typical. I owe him a paper about it. Except that I've been distracted and distraught by hormones and dark forces. Again.

The blank page sneers at me. Okay, it isn't exactly blank. So far I've drawn a tiny camel, a bear, a snake and several scorpions. I diligently make more scorpions who shoot fire out of their butts at the tiny humans who run away screaming and on fire. I'd be willing to run out of this class screaming and on fire, trust me.

But the main guy in the book we are reading hasn't even shot anybody yet, but you can tell he is thinking about it.

So right now I am drawing a small passenger plane, maybe six or eight seats. It's belching smoke like the girls' bathroom between classes, and careening over the Sahara desert. Should I let it land nicely and everyone goes to a pleasant lunch? Or should I crash it into some huge sand dune and then see what happens next? Maybe some people will survive. Humans are annoying that way. And Laila is definitely on this plane. Maybe I can rescue her.

Chapter 2

It was barely dawn when Dash Lahlou handed his grandmother the loaf of fresh *khobz* from the communal oven. It bore their family's mark, so there could be no mistake. The perfume of cinnamon and almonds was a daily reminder of his idyllic life.

Today would be a good day to ride his dirt bike, Dash decided, as he washed down the the bread and fruit with hot mint tea. There would be some great new dunes on the edge of the Sahara, where the eastern foothills of the Atlas mountains fought their eternal battle against the sand.

None of his buddies could go, but all his chores were caught up, so he would just go on his own. His grandma had no complaints about Dash. In fact, she spoiled him rotten. He could get a couple of hours in on his dirt bike before the sun got high.

An hour later, Dash stopped at the top of a dune to drink water. His motorcycle, a small 1970's Kawasaki, was running great.

He heard it before he saw it, an unhappy, intermittent buzzing from the south-east. He squinted against the sun. Smoke. It was a two engine plane with twin fins on the tail, maybe a Beechcraft, or an old AVRO, one engine was smoking and the other was thinking about it. It was too low and headed towards the mountains behind him. That made no sense, the plane had no altitude. In fact, it was losing. Now it looked like the pilot was planning to park it in the sand.

"Nose up!" Dash whispered to himself, not that he knew anything about flying, but that was what they always said in books and movies. Sudden silence behind the wind. The pilot must have shut off the remaining engine. The plane's belly hit the first dune and bounced, the second hit spun it on an angle and the tip of a wing snapped off. The plane bounced high again and then plunged nose first into a cloud of sand.

Dash started his engine and headed carefully down the dune. He was met by the eerie ticking of stressed hot metal. Dash dropped his bike 50 meters away in case the plane did explode. He ran to the plane and pulled open the pilot's door. He was slumped forward, the windshield glass was cracked. Dash felt his neck. No pulse. There was no co-pilot. Dash climbed over the body and into the cabin. There were four rows of two seats on each side. There were two men and a girl. A young man in a western business suit was dead too. An older man, also in a suit, was moaning. His seat had broken and a leg twisted under him awkwardly. The girl had her head, wrapped in scarves, between her knees, sobbing. He touched the back of her neck.

"Miss, are you injured?"

She lifted her head. She was wearing sunglasses which she did not remove. "My father?"

"I think his leg is broken. I'm no doctor."

"Ahmed? The young guy?"

"Dead, like your pilot."

"Papa!?" The girl twisted in her seat. Dash tried to help her up. As the tail of the plane was pointed up in the air at about a 30 degree angle it was difficult.

"Don't touch me!"

"O...kay..." Dash turned away to help the man. Dash cut the seat belt with his pocket knife and dragged him by the armpits, stopping only to open the fuselage door. It was a hard drop to the sand.

"I can help," the man groaned.

Dash jumped down and yelled. "Fall into my arms."

"Can you get Laila and Ahmed out first?"

"There's just one door, and you're in it."

The man fell on top of Dash and they both collapsed, the man screamed.

Dash climbed back into the plane. Through a window he could see a glittering stream of clear liquid dripping. Av gas and hot metal. This might not end well. Metal creaked beneath him.

"Are you coming, Miss?"

"Laila. What about our luggage?"

"Luggage?" Maybe she was in shock.

"It's Vuitton," she said, like that was an explanation.

"It's what?" Dash just stared at her and then took out his pocket knife again and cut the seat belt straps.

He needed something straight and stiff to use as a splint for her father's leg. The luggage was strewn about.

"Miss, we need to go."

"Ahmed will help – 'Ahmed!'" she called out.

"Ah... I don't think so."

Dash went back to the bodies. He took the wallet and cell phone of the pilot and the plane's log book. Then Ahmed's wallet and cell. It was grisly business, robbing the dead. The Ahmed person had a dark hole in his chest, the shirt soaked in blood. Dash realized Ahmed had been shot. This was now more interesting.

"Miss! Just jump, the sand is soft. That's why you're alive."

Laila jumped, and was only partially successful in keeping her dress from lifting up. Nice long legs, Dash thought.

Dash noticed a piece of plastic trim. It looked fairly rigid. Dash tore it away from the luggage bin, he could shorten it later.

He landed on the sand and dropped to his knees.

"We have to get away from the plane. Grab one of your father's shoulders."

They did that. The girl was pretty useless. When they got to Dash's bike he stopped and looked back. It was then he saw more bullet holes stretching across the fuselage and wing. What the hell? Who were these people?

"Our luggage?" Laila reproached him with her chin.

"You're welcome," Dash muttered as he went back down the dune.

Dash was happy to leave them at the first scruffy tree. The climbing had been rotten in the heat and soft sand. He gave them his water, and instructions to keep the man's leg above his heart. He used the stiff plastic and strips of airplane seat belts for a makeshift splint. It wasn't great. He stood up and wiped his forehead.

"I'll be back in an hour."

Laila was staring into her cell, not believing. "No phone service?"

Dash stared at her.

"Then how do we get help?" Laila demanded, still not looking up.

"I am the help."

"I want a proper doctor. Not some voodoo medicine man."

"Me get-um big chief," Dash snapped back.

The father grabbed Dash's hand with both of his. His eyes were fevered.

"If they come... if they come... she is my angel, my life, but..."

"If who comes?" Dash leaned closer, glancing sideways to see if Laila had heard. The man's voice was weak, but he reared up.

"Promise me! If they come, you have to kill her. Promise me!"

Chapter 3

Dash made himself busy putting the phones and wallets in the small saddlebag on his dirt bike, where he kept his lunch and spare plugs and a few tools. The father must have hit his head, that would explain his crazy talk.

Thirty minutes later Dash slid his bike into the shed and set the kick-stand. He grunted as he took the car battery off the shelf and put it into his father's ancient Land Rover, tightening up the brace. He checked the oil. The truck roared to life. He threw piece of wood in the back. It would make a better splint than plastic.

Dash ran in to their house tell his grandmother what had happened and to grab more water. As he stepped outside he saw a younger boy, about twelve, holding a soccer ball.

"Addi! Tell your mother you're coming to help me! There's a plane crash."

"We heard the noise!" Addi wasn't missing that, and five minutes later they had left The Oasis and were speeding down the mountain on a single lane dirt road. Soon they would be at the true desert. The transitions of nature in their country were often sudden and astonishing. Dash looked at his watch. He had been gone one hour. Not bad. Another ten minutes. Addi badgered him with questions, none of which Dash answered.

"This is the help?" Laila stared at Addi in dismay. "My father is the Minister of the Interior! You should have brought proper help! What's wrong with you!? We are injured... and late... and... and inconvenienced!"

Addi looked at Dash, who just shrugged.

"All the men are away, working," Dash explained. "It would have taken longer to get someone. Anyway, the truck only holds four, and your father has to keep his leg straight."

They maneuvered the Minister of the Interior sideways into the back seat. Laila sat in the front, and Addi sat on the luggage in the back, holding on to the roll bar that held the canvas top in place.

"Hold on Addi!" Dash yelled. "I can't come back if you fall off."

"Ha!" was all Addi had to say, knowing full well any of the village boys could walk home from where they were. They knew these foothills and the edge of the Sahara since the time they could walk.

Normally Dash would have tried to bounce Addi, but now he had to be careful. He stole a sideways glance at this Laila and her sun glasses and bright silk scarf. She stared straight ahead. Dash looked too, frowning. There was a narrow dirt road that tracked the edge of the desert and then turned up into the foothills. Scrub changed to lush greenery. What was she staring at?

"Where were you flying from?" Dash asked as casually as he could, rather than saying *"Why is your plane full of freakin' bullet holes?"*

"Tasili n Ajjer – I had a photo shoot with Teen Vogue... and the Algerian Tourist Bureau."

Dash knew of the place, though he had never been there. Plateau of the Rivers. In the south-east corner of Algeria, on the borders of Libya and Niger, on the far side of the Sahara, it was known for having thousands of spectacular millennia-old petroglyphs.

"Do cell phones work in your village? What was your name again?"

"Same as it was five minutes, ago, right Dash?" Addi giggled. Laila was too much for him, too.

"Elders will drive your father to the hospital in Béchar tomorrow. You will be able to telephone whomever you wish from there."

"Tomorrow?"

"Tonight you will be our guests."

"How can you not have cell phones?"

"We have managed without them for a thousand years," Dash smiled. "Anyway, if we want to see someone we just walk over to their house and see them. Right Addi? Did I need a telephone to find you today?"

"I want a cell phone!" Addi's white teeth gleamed under curly dark hair.

"What for? Who would you call? You see everyone you know every day, right?"

"I would order American pizza," Addi decided, and even Laila laughed.

Chapter 4

The elders had taken over the rescue on their arrival, Dash had given them the wallets, phones and log book. Dash had not seen the guests again and had just played football with the kids, eaten, and gone to bed early. One day of Laila and her father had been exhausting.

It was midnight when his grandma woke him from a deep contented sleep. He stumbled out into the common area of the village as she pressed a cup of hot sweet mint tea into his hands. He drank it, trying to wake up. The village elders were still standing around the snapping fire, talking quietly to Laila's father. Someone had found an ancient pair of wooden crutches for him, that must be why they were all standing, out of courtesy.

Usually they sat, laughing, telling stories long into the cold night. Stories of those who had passed through their village on the way to their fates. It was deemed by consensus, over many years and generations, that no one ever outran their fate.

The Oasis surrounded a natural spring in a narrow valley in the Atlas mountains on the east side of the border that divided Algeria and Morocco. It was a place of repose with plenty of shade, fresh fruit and rest. They grew dates and almonds, raised sheep, goats and chickens and produced argan oil to be made into beauty products. Some of the women worked silver obtained by labor or trade, enabling the village to get what it needed from the outside world. The men mostly worked on the Mediterranean coast, at a new de-salinization plant, and would come home every few months. There was also smuggling through the mountains because officially the border between

Algeria and Morocco was closed, and had been for many years. This was an activity in which Dash's uncles had engaged in better days, but in recent years rebels, bandits, government patrols, war and worse had made it increasingly difficult and less profitable.

On a modern map (for which the villagers cared little) their village was in Algeria, but racially they were Berber, an ancient people who had partially succumbed to Arab expansion in the seventh century. Visitors over the centuries had been Arab, Spanish, French, Russian, and even German and British during the second world war. Those who made it this far from the world, dehydrated, starved and exhausted, had had any animosity beaten out of them by nature, and were grateful for the refuge. No one had ever dishonored their hosts during their stay. Even during times of war between Morocco and Algeria, and Morocco and the Western Sahara their village had sheltered wounded and deserters from all sides. Their world was small - their village, their valley, protected by mountains - and their past.

Dash Lahlou didn't think about any of this. He thought tonight about his own father, who should have been standing there by the fire as one of the elders, and his beautiful mother who stroked his hair and was so proud of him.

After independence from France, Dash's grandfather had been considered too friendly to the pied noir and the occupying government. That he owned French books and was accused of speaking French in public had been proof enough of his guilt. Many of his books had been burned as an example to the other villages to deny hospitality to the colonials. In the end, most of the surviving pied noir had returned to Europe. The stain of bitterness lasted a long time.

That was before Dash was born, but he knew the story well. His own parents were currently stuck in Morocco, the city of Tangiers, an important port town on the Mediterranean, across from Gibraltar, where they had gone to deliver a shipment of silver jewelry and uncut stones. It was their largest, most expensive venture into the world, but his parents had been unable to return due to a flare-up of terror that was sweeping everywhere like an evil wind. The cities were targets for cowardly bombings and assassinations, the country villages targets for raids, massacres and especially the thievery of children and young women.

Dash's father too was known as an intellectual and modernist, too interested in western ideas. He had been a professor of history at University 1 when Dash was young, but his political sympathies as a reformer had made many enemies, and he had retreated to their ancestral village to wait for the political wind to change. He hosted sympathetic visitors and refugees. Their campfire discussions would go long into the night.

Years ago there had been a Catholic priest who had set up a school, teaching French, Spanish, English and mathematics, but the priest had left on short notice, taken by the elders to a train many miles away before he could be harmed. Since those days the village kept its head down. They enjoyed the visitors and traders, they were hospitable by nature, not political.

Before that there had been a Foreign Legion outpost nearby, though now it was a ruin. The soldiers had given the children footballs and bought some of their food from the village. The rebels who hid in the mountains even then had threatened to punish the village, but they too needed supplies to survive and The Oasis was respected as a neutral zone.

It is doubtful if the villagers knew much if anything about Switzerland, but that was what they were, a tiny Switzerland in the eastern foothills of the Atlas mountains, as they had been for hundreds, maybe a thousand years. Conquests, politics and imperial ambition came and went, the villagers waited stoically for the worst to pass.

Dash's grandmother pressed an old khaki backpack into his arms. There was German script stenciled on one of the flaps. Then she opened her hand and on a soft dark cloth were sprinkled a few small loose gem stones and a worked silver bracelet. Dash stared into her eyes. He did not understand what this gift meant, but he knew it was ominous. He stood by the fire. He slipped on the bracelet.

Laila's father, M. de la Finistere, Minister of the Interior, leaned on his crutches, staring. His face at that moment seemed carved and ancient as the flames flickered across it. His dark beard was trimmed under a sharp nose and restless dark eyes. A handsome, important man encountering doubt for perhaps the first time.

"After today, it is not safe for Laila to stay with me," Finestere's head sagged. "Many senior officials are targets for bribery, kidnapping and assassination."

"Send her on an airplane to safety," someone suggested. "Send her back to America."

"There are too many spies in the government department which handles visas," said another.

The debate went on. Finally the most senior elder, a tall man with fierce eyes and a long silver beard, spoke. "It is decided. Dash will take her through the mountains to meet her Uncle, Taha de la Finestere."

"What?" Dash said, astonished at the sound of his own voice. He was not one to talk back to his elders, but this was ridiculous.

Everyone stared, as if surprised he was even there.

"It's too dangerous," Dash said quietly.

"You will have to take the old way." Silver Beard shrugged. "I did it myself in my youth."

"Not with a... a girl... a girl you didn't!" Dash muttered, using a colloquial expression referencing the rear end of a female sheep.

"You will deliver her to the Uncle Taha, on the Atlantic coast of Morocco, and when she is safe, you will return. Also – make no sounds in the Forest of Storms."

He made it sound so simple. And the Forest of Storms? That was a campfire story from childhood about trees that shot lightning at you.

Monsieur queried the elders vigorously, not caring that Dash was right there, as to his suitability for such a task.

He is the best available, the elders said. Experienced in the mountains and clever. Anyway, the more mature young men were not there.

No matter how important his daughter was, there was no one else to send.

Chapter 5

"Yes, Dashiell?" Mr. Mulch stared at my raised hand.

"I have diarrhea, Sir."

"Last time it was black death, or the plague, if memory serves," Mr. Mulch said dryly. He says everything dryly.

"It's the cafeteria, Sir." I shifted my weight from leg to leg for effect. "I have a sensitive stomach."

He excused me with a wave of disgust.

Diarrhea? Have it? I can't even spell it. I opened the emergency door at the end of the hall and took the foil from a gum wrapper and folded it, slipping it into into the door jamb so the lock wouldn't click shut. If the guys who designed schools designed prisons they would all be empty.

Then I leaned against my favorite wall in the stair well and thought what was the deal with the Swedish back-packer guy who had just transferred in. His name was Lucas, but I called him Sven because it annoyed him. He wore his blonde hair long and tied in dreadlocks. When the Jamaicans do that it is cool, but when Sven does it he looks like an idiot. But the girls fuss over him and he gets mad when they dress too slutty—which is every day—so he must be exhausted. Why was Sven in Detention? Probably just showed up to get Laila's Snap. Crap. Wish I'd thought of that.

My phone buzzed. Crap. Mr. Mulch.

"Dashiell, you can't take extended breaks, or this wouldn't be detention. I don't mean to inconvenience you..."

"It's not inconvenient Sir, it's diarrhea... I'm doing my best, Sir."

"Well, there is no nurse here today..."

"Yes sir."

Crap. Another F lurking. Should I go and write the stupid test? Does it count? My parents are cool as long as I have straight B's. Maybe I should transfer. If I were in a different class than Laila I might get some work done. But then she'd have no protection from Sven, the fake Swede. Doesn't Sven realize that without short skirts and crop-tops school would be even more boring and unbearable?

Chapter 6

An hour later Dash was taken into a guest house where the Minister of the Interior, lay, his leg raised on cushions. A ceiling fan spun.

"We gave him morphine..." one of the grannies nursing him giggled as they left to make tea.

"That stuff's ancient!" Dash whispered.

"You may call me Monsieur de la Finistere. You have some French?" He frowned.

"En peut, Monsieur."

"What does your father do?"

"My father was a Professor of History at University 1 - and served in the previous government."

"Previous government?" Finestere smiled grimly.

"My father loves our country, he wanted only to serve." Dash was surprised at the sound of his own voice. "He did not participate in the sins of our past. And it cost him his job."

"I know who your father is, an idealist, but I have no grievance with him. And you were not even born in the worst of it," Laila's father now looked at Dash with more curiosity. Dash felt tremendous anxiety.

"What do you know of the world, Dash?" Finestere's eyes flashed.

"I listen to the elders at night, Sir. I read. I'm still a student. I know I have a lot to learn."

"What do you know of revolution? Fevered. Dark. Turning on itself like a snake trying to devour its own tail... even here in paradise." He gestured absently. "Your little village is like the Palm Springs of Algeria. Go to school, study marketing, get some tourists in here. You have a hot spring, a cold fresh water spring! Palm trees and flowers. Open a spa!"

Dash did not respond. He knew the voice of morphine.

"Our friends in Morocco do not want to import either revolution or refugees. Can you blame them? They have been secretly building walls in areas where the mountains are not sufficient."

"Not so secretly, Sir." Dash said. "Every one has seen them. Yet they want access to our oil."

"Yes. I'm impressed that you know this. What do you think?"

"At a fair price, anything is possible."

"Exactly."

"What is our government's position?"

"That we have a more immediate problem than haggling in the medina over oil and mining rights. Rebels come to the far villages, they take women and children to be slaves for their fighters and then disappear. Any elders who object are executed. There is no option, no reasoning with them. They move quickly and are gone. Our army hunts them, as do the Moroccans, but they are many and quick, they know intimately the no-man's lands and trails of the Sahara. And our armies are not allowed to cross the borders, so they laugh at us from the other side.

None of this was news to Dash. He was not sure if he was the focus of this speech or if monsieur had forgotten he was even there and was addressing some imagined parliament.

"One of Laila's uncles – my elder brother - was a venerable holy man," He continued. "...he made prophecies about her before he himself was... murdered. He claimed her to be the perfect descendant of Dihya." He squinted at Dash.

"She was the Berber warrior priestess who led armies against the Arabs in the 7th Century."

"Again I see that you have some education. As for Dihya, the Arabs too knew her, as al-Kahini, priestess, warrior and soothsayer who could tell the future."

"Can Laila tell the future?" Dash asked, hoping there was some redemptive quality to this girl if he was going to get stuck with her.

"She *is* the future - pass me that bag."

Dash reached for an ancient leather satchel. It was heavy.

Laila's father rummaged through it and then pressed something wrapped in an oily cloth into Dash's hand. It was a MAC 50, a small automatic pistol favored by the French Foreign Legion in the colonial days. So it was at least 60 years old. This was serious. Dash felt the weight of it in his heart as he had never felt anything since his parents left.

He had stared at snow in the Atlas mountains just that very morning. He did not have the right gear, that was just a fact.

"Monsieur..." Dash began. "What you said to me this morning... at the crash site... you were just in shock, right?"

"Please, light me a cigarette." Finestere nodded at the table.

Dash held the match carefully.

"It's your job, it's your duty and responsibility to make sure you never have to make that decision. Take her for a long walk. Deliver her to Taha, my brother... and I will be in your debt. Not a bad situation for a young man, to have a friend at court." Finestere raised an eyebrow but did not smile.

Dash stuffed the gun in the back of his pants and turned to go.

"Who was the boy who helped this morning?"

"Addi?"

"He will go with you and Laila."

"He's a kid. I'll have enough trouble with..." Dash stopped himself.

"He will sleep in the middle."

"Addi's just a kid."

"He will sleep in the middle. That is his job - to sleep in the middle, maybe help collect water and wood, but mostly to sleep in the middle. Send him to me now."

"I didn't know that was a job."

"Send the boy to me."

Dash left the room. The night sky was fresh and sparkling as he looked up. His life playing football with his friends, riding his dirt bike, working in the gardens, caring for the goats, reading his father's library and eating his grandmother's wonderful food, it was all disappearing before his eyes. He went and embraced his grandma, a tiny bird-like woman with endless energy and a bottomless heart.

Chapter 7

Welcome to my daily suck-i-tude. Who gives detention on a Saturday? But I've rescued Laila, that's got to be worth something. And Dash's village is pretty nice. I drew lots of palm trees and a waterfall and you can see the Atlas Mountains with snow on the peaks from there.

Then I am struck by a genius idea. I am going to write the craziest story I can think of. Laila is going to be in it, with her looks how could she not be? And the stupid Swede. And a bunch of other people you haven't met yet. Some of them will be cool, though.

And Dash. He'll be my alter-ego. He'll be super-flex and IF he behaves he'll get to be with Laila. Which is why I hate him and why I'm going to make him suffer. I am going to make Dash suffer. What's the worst stuff I can do to him?

First of all I'm going to make Laila only sixteen. A sophomore. Jailbait. And snakes. Something bad with snakes. And scorpions, which are way cooler than snakes. I sharpen my pencil and stare at Laila for inspiration.

Chapter 8

Laila's almond-shaped eyes stared at the ground. She clasped a blanket about her shoulders and her face was in shadow. Her demeanor invited nothing, they might have been discussing the fate of someone else.

Dash could not tell her appearance except that she was tall and slender. He looked at her feet. American sneakers, certainly not adequate. Dash was told that she spoke several dialects, Arabic and French, but preferred English. Well, too bad. Dash had no English except for fashionable swear words and scraps from movies.

For that moment she was silent. She stared at Dash with annoyance, when she thought he wasn't looking.

Dash didn't care. He turned his back on her and went back to his room. They had to be up at dawn.

Of course he could not sleep. He went through his things, books, a pre-Calculus textbook, a knife with an engraved silver handle. There were wolves in the mountains. He had an old bolt-action rifle he used for hunting game birds. He would leave that for his friends who would take care of things until he returned.

In the end he took only the knife. He did not anticipate that he would need books to traverse the Atlas Mountains.

He sat on the edge of his bed and deftly sewed the gems into the waistband of his pants. He hoped he would not need them.

Dash longed to go to school, study. He wanted to be a doctor, learn the large world and live in peace. In his mind, the life of a soldier was nothing to aspire to. He ran his finger along the edge of his knife.

Chapter 9

Dawn came too fast. Laila's father now stood, leaning on his wooden crutches, in front of Dash as they prepared to leave. His mood had not improved, but he was less delirious than earlier. He gave a long list of instructions to which Dash listened respectfully, but to him they had little to do with anything.

"Do you understand?"

"Yes, sir."

"I do not have to tell you that Laila must be protected with your life – and that her honor must be intact at the destination. You are not even to look upon her and you are certainly not to touch her. Even better, have her walk behind you."

Finistere held Dash's gaze but Dash did not look away.

"I have no other words for you, except that if you succeed I will be forever in your debt, and if you fail I will curse you beyond the grave. No man puts himself in debt to another unless the cause is blessed."

"You are sending me into the mountains with a kid, an old gun and a young girl?" Dash opened his hands in a gesture of emptiness. "I will do my best, but you should say your good-byes to her now. The most I can promise you, is that if we are to be taken prisoner, I agree with you. She will not be dishonored, for I will kill her myself first."

Dash may just as well have slapped him, but Finistere said nothing. He knew what he had asked.

Dash was a respectful young man, but he was upset. This man was from the Mediterranean cities, he had no idea. To cross the mountains to the Atlantic coast on foot was difficult in good times. With rebels and regular bandits everywhere? They would have to go at the highest possible altitude to be safe. Certainly they did not have the right equipment for a winter passage.

Dash did not wait for a response. He turned and went to take leave of his grandmother and the elders, and to remind them to explain to his parents why he would not be here to greet them when he returned. They made the customary prayers for the journey. They should have made extra.

Chapter 10

"Why don't you have soldiers to take me? Men. Not a...a... boy and *him*?" Laila asked after they had been walking for about two hours. Addi had run ahead, collecting sticks, delighted to be out of school.

"I would like soldiers, too," Dash set a quicker pace. "Then I could be home living my happy life and not here listening to you complain!"

"When do we rest?" Laila asked, after they had walked perhaps another five minutes.

"We could go back to the village and rest, and start again tomorrow."

Laila removed her sunglasses to shoot another fiery glance.

"I'll make you walk 10 paces behind me, like in the old days," Dash snapped. "I didn't ask for this job."

But he waited for her to catch up.

"Thank you," she said, not looking at him.

"We can rest fifteen minutes every two hours," Dash offered.

"Thank you. I've been sitting on my butt in school and then on planes. Not used to walking."

"When did you come from America?"

"A couple of days ago. I had to get up in the middle of the night, I couldn't even say goodbye to my friends."

"Why didn't they just fly you to Casablanca or Rabat?"

"There are spies. Father always says I am at risk of being kidnapped."

"Your story makes no sense. If I were your family, I would have left you safe in America."

"Well, that shows what you know. I am here for a reason."

"Must be some big-ass reason." Addi chirped, having burned off a little of his excess energy.

Laila took out ear buds from her back pack and put them on, quickening her pace.

"Addi, I see why you are so popular with girls."

"I know."

An hour later Dash signaled to stop. Addi dropped his pack and deftly made a fire for tea.

Laila sat and groaned and finally removed her ear buds.

"Why are you going to Morocco?" Addi asked.

"I am to help my father negotiate and organize cooperation between Algeria and Morocco to fight the rebels and help the refugees of both countries.

"How are you going to do this? We cannot negotiate anything with Morocco! We have been trying for a generation."

"I am going to tour the villages that have been hit by the rebels, distribute relief supplies, and comfort and encourage the people..." Laila began. "My father is planning the supplies and security, and it is better if I am out of the way until they are ready. Each minister is a target... and I am going to change my clothes," Laila unwound her *khimar*. "Up here in the mountains, there are only you boys."

"You should pray there is only us," Dash admonished her. "If we meet some rabid dogs on the trail, your modesty will not save us. We should chop your hair and make you look like Addi."

"Like a handsome young boy?" Laila smiled and Addi blushed, and spun and then fell down.

Dash groaned. "Your father instructed that you are to walk behind me, and I am never to look at you."

Laila, to Dash's surprise, laughed. "But you have already looked at me. So already you have screwed up. So considering that, do I look like a boy?"

"No, you look like an annoying city girl."

"Why did you say I look like a boy?"

"I said you *should* look like a boy. It would be safer if we get in trouble."

Laila softened her tone. "What education do you have?"

Dash and Addi turned their backs on her while she changed.

"I have mathematics and French. I will take my bacca when my father returns."

"You don't look like a brain. You look like a typical foot-baller."

"You look like a girl who just wants to go to the mall."

"What's a mall, Dash?" Laila teased.

"I know! I know!" Addi interjected.

Laila and Dash both stared at him.

"A bunch of shops with a roof and a common food area," Addi tossed smugly.

"A food court, they call it—okay—how do I look?" Laila asked.

Dash turned. Laila preened. Slender, wearing a hoodie, ripped jeans, her hair falling loosely almost to her waist. She looked entirely American except her skin had the copper glow of pure Berber blood offset by flashing eyes. Even Addi was silenced.

"Have either of you ever been to a mall?" She challenged them.

"No." Dash admitted. "But I know it is a place for the purchase of frivolous things from China."

"And here. Argan oil for beauty products. I know your village produces it. One of my favorite things to do in America is to show friends pictures of the goats in the trees. Let's go," Laila marched off ahead of him, as if she knew exactly where they were going.

Dash let her and Addi go ahead, but he soon caught up, even her long legs were no match for his.

"My father and his party in the government believe that the rebels are a profound threat to all of North Africa, in fact, the only way to defeat them quickly is to unite the Algerian and Moroccan people, Berber and Arab and everyone, to distract us from our differences. I will be promoted as the Berber descendent of Dihya. There will be many government reforms and a broadening of democracy in both Algeria and Morocco, though Morocco is ahead of us in this. I will help promote our shared interests as our strength. This will give the governments of North Africa an excuse to work together without losing face with our traditional citizens, and combine our resources to defeat the rebels."

"Nice speech. And you left America to do this?"

"You met my father. He believes it is necessary. If he can sacrifice so much, how can I do nothing?"

Her eyes pleaded with Dash to understand.

"If this is so important, why are they sending me? Even I know this is ridiculous. If we run into a rebel patrol, we have no chance, I tell you, none."

"I was not told why it had to be... you..." Laila stared at Dash, frustrated, trying to imagine what had compelled her father to have chosen this boy with a pretty face, rather than a man who would command respect. "Do you even shave? Are you trained as a soldier?"

"No. I have shot birds. But I have never killed a person," Dash began. "In fact, I have no ambition to kill a person, and if I can live my entire life having killed no person, I will not feel diminished in any way. But I promised your father I would take you safely, and I will do my best."

"Then pray that we are lucky and can walk to our destination without adventure. Pass me to uncle Taha and you are free."

"Have you met him?"

"Who? My uncle? Of course."

"Recently? Can he protect you?"

"It was a few years ago," Laila admitted. "As I told you I have been in America for the past three years. Have you ever been on the internet? I have often talked to Taha on the internet."

"I've been to an internet café with my father," Dash said with pride. He had seen the images moving on a flat piece of glass, but he had not communicated with anyone inside the glass.

"My uncle is an advisor to the King in Morocco. He is a liaison. They have a plan. To show unity to the people, between the King and our government in Algiers. There will be reforms in both countries. I will be the face of comfort to the people."

Dash nodded but said nothing. He knew country people his whole life. Friendly, generous, but also wary, suspicious. Fierce in their loyalty, but that ferocity also extended to their prejudices and superstitions. It was not easy to convince them of anything.

The trail was now so narrow that they had to walk single file, to their right was a steep drop of at least a thousand meters.

"Where are we going that the trail has to be so bad?" Laila asked.

"This isn't bad – yet. We are going to a village where we will sleep tonight – as guests. They won't know who you are, so you should wear your *khimar* for respect. We are old-fashioned in the mountains. It will be our last night of relative comfort. And this narrow trail is chosen because it is safer. Rebels, bandits, smugglers - they travel with pack animals, donkeys, so they are not burdened and can fight. They do not go on these narrow paths, and neither do their prey. These routes are only for those who are afraid."

"Are we afraid?" Laila asked.

"We had better be."

"I'm not afraid of anything!" Addi chirped. "What's that noise?"

"You have never come this far, Addi?" Dash asked. "It's the rapids before the Forest of Storms."

"The elder said not to go this way."

"The elder is, um... elder. This is much faster, and safe as long as we are quiet."

They peered across the ancient, moss covered wooden bridge and down into the violent, foaming water a hundred meters below, crashing against sharp and ancient stones.

"I'm scared, I'll admit it," Laila offered.

"I'll go first. There is one trick, we go one at a time, slowly, then there is no one to jiggle the ropes – and anything green is slippery."

Addi and Laila exchanged worried glances, happy to let Dash go first.

"The ropes are wet, you have to hold on," Dash yelled over his shoulder, half way across. A black bird landed in front of him, and then took off again. The bridge shook under Dash's weight.

Then he was across. Laila went next and finally Addi, determined to look brave in front of Dash and this girl. Addi fell to his knees dramatically once he was across. "Yeah!" He yelled.

"Addi!" Dash raised a finger to his lips. "This is the Forest of Storms ahead! No noise."

"Sorry!"

The air thinned as they climbed, and there was less energy for conversation. They stared up at the dead and barren black-barked trees. They looked burned, but there was no new undergrowth, and Dash had always been told that they were ancient. And silent. No birds, no flowers, no nothing.

Laila was struggling.

"Stop," Dash whispered as he reached for her back pack.

Laila spun and grabbed Dash's arm and suddenly Dash was on the ground, flat on his back.

"Umph," the air came out of his chest. "I was offering to take some of your gear," Dash jumped back up to his feet.

"I didn't hear you. Please don't touch me."

"Fine. Carry your own stuff. And walk behind me from now on…"

"That was cool," Addi smiled. "Show me…"

The crack of lightning made them all deaf and blinded for a moment. The tree trunk it had split was ten meters away. The smell of burnt wood and electricity was strong.

"Let's keep going," Dash whispered.

"This place is spooky," Addi said and walked closer to Dash.

In another hour there was green scrub again, they were out of the Forest of Storms.

Dash put up his hand to stop and whispered "I smell something. Something bad."

Soon they all smelled the faint, sickening smoke. they turned a corner and and saw the plumes on the next ridge, looking over a narrow valley.

It took them another hour to reach the village, wrapping their faces in scarves to help filter the smell. Several bodies lay in a row in an open area. Some of the buildings were burning also.

There was no one running with water. The only survivors were old men and women and children less than ten years old. A few scattered single shot rifles were stacked against a tree.

Dash turned to Laila and Addi, "You can wait at those rocks where we turned. Here, take my back-pack. You don't have to see this."

"I need to see this," Laila's voice quivered, but her eyes were strong.

Dash shrugged and turned. "Addi - I'm warning you."

"How long ago?" Dash asked the surviving elder Hassan, whom he knew, who was leaning his back against a tree. He was gut-shot, and his wife was giving him water.

"The sun was high."

"How many soldiers?"

"Many. Perhaps six."

"How many did they take?"

"The girls old enough to bleed. The boys old enough to walk for one day - like him." He pointed at Addi, who did not look quite so brave at that moment.

"The number that were taken?"

"Maybe a dozen."

"Which way did they go, the devil ones?"

"To the west, the easy trail. You can catch them. How many are you?"

"Three."

Hassan stared blankly.

"Can you survive, the remaining?" Dash asked.

The elder looked past him. "They took so much. I had to beg for petrol to burn the bodies. Then they shot me for asking."

"Do you know who I am?"

"You are the promised one - but you have come too late," Hassan said, his voice trailing away.

"In the morning," Dash began, "have your people gather blankets and what food they can and go to The Oasis. It is two days walking for you, I think. Mostly downhill. Your people can do it."

"I knew your grandfather - can you take us?"

"I have to go to the west."

"Where they are? To rescue our grandchildren?"

"No, I am sorry. I will avoid the devil ones. I will take the smugglers' path."

Laila glared at Dash, then approached the old man and stroked his face with her fingers. His eyes closed, but he spoke to Dash.

"Will you at least kill them for us? Death is not enough, but it is something."

"No. I will avoid them."

"Are you not the one who was promised?"

"No, I am not the one who was promised," Dash sighed. He wanted to help Hassan, but he did not want to lie. "I have faith that God will send one to punish those who have betrayed him and taken his children. I pray it will be soon."

The man nodded.

"But I am not he."

"I have prayed, but God does not hear me anymore," the elder grimaced in pain. "My wife will give you water," he said. "Can you take away my pain before you go?" he asked. "I have already said good-bye."

Laila stared at Dash in new horror.

"I'm sorry."

"Please?" The wife made a gesture. "He can never make it to your village. Let him die at home and be buried with his ancestors."

Dash took out the gun Laila's father had given him, made sure there was a shell in the chamber and gave it to Hassan.

The man took the gun with gratitude and pressed it against his head and closed his eyes.

Click.

"God is not ready for you yet. I am sorry, my friend."

Dash patted the man on the shoulder as he took the gun back. He turned to look for Laila, that they should leave, but she was walking ahead. The wailing and weeping of the women diminished a little as Laila knelt beside each one and stroked their faces with her fingers. They stayed there for a long time, trying to comfort those who could not be comforted. Addi ran back and forth with water, but his eyes were burdened. Dash hated for Addi to see this. Then the shadows were long and they had to go. They would camp upwind.

As soon as they were alone, Laila turned to Dash. "We have to rescue those children."

Dash and Addi both stared at her in astonishment. "How?"

Laila's eyes flared. "We have to try."

"We are kids, with one gun between us that doesn't even work. If you want to die or be sold in the slave market we can go stumbling down the trail after them. Or we can complete our journey and report what happened to the authorities. They can send soldiers. That group is not moving fast."

Laila's pretty lips were pressed tightly as she walked ahead of him without responding. Addi stared but said nothing.

As soon as they found a good spot upwind of the burning village they pitched camp. One tarp, three sleeping bags, three back packs of supplies. Addi was diligent with the wood, it would be cold tonight.

They worked without speaking, lost in the horror of what they had seen. Their tradition was for bodies to be buried, not burned. But there was no one to give the dead their comfort by putting them properly in tombs.

As they settled by the fire to eat, Laila spoke. "Did my father give you that weapon?"

"Yes."

"He doesn't know anything about guns."

"Neither do I."

"Why you?" Addi asked Laila bluntly. "What makes you so great?"

"Because..." she paused, "I will tell you the craziness that I have surrendered to. They all think I am the incarnation of the warrior goddess, Dihya, or al-Kahina, as the Arabs call her. It's a long story."

"Is that why you were in Tasili n Ajjer? Dash asked. "It wasn't Teen Vogue."

"It was both. I can do more than one thing at a time, Dash. Photographing images of some ancient archeological sites to promote the common heritage of the North African people."

They drank the hot mint tea. "We don't believe in that, in Goddesses." Dash frowned.

"I'm just telling you what I have been told since I was little. And in the villages, the countryside. They believe. In the cities too, Dash. Arabs and Berbers alike, all over north Africa, grew up with the story. You would be surprised."

"Those stories are for children," Dash said. "My parents believe in education, and always said that the old superstitions and primitive religion is what held our people back. What did Dihya do that was so great?"

"Do you truly want to know?"

"Sure," Dash shrugged.

"Dihya agreed to marry an evil king in exchange for freedom for her people," Laila paused. "Then, on her wedding night, she came to his bed and slit his throat." Laila laughed at the shock on Dash's face. It was a sparkling, beautiful laugh.

Addi looked a bit green.

"Well that's, um, ah... romantic," Dash smiled. "Drink your tea, knife lady."

Dash used a stick to pull three large stones from the fire and wrapped them in pieces of old cloth.

"This is how you stay warm," he placed one in the bottom of Laila's sleeping bag. "Keep your feet on it - Addi, you sleep in the middle."

"I hear my father in your voice."

"You got that."

"Thank you, this is warm." Laila tried to get comfortable, using her backpack as a pillow, staring up at the stars. "I'm sorry Dash, I know you are not a soldier, it's just that when I think of those children..."

"Their fate is not set in stone, if we can complete our journey quickly and report the attack, there will be time."

"Is your village safe, Dash?"

Dash sat by the fire. "I used to think so."

Chapter 11

Dash awoke at first light and renewed the fire. It was cold. Laila was asleep, with Addi curled up against her like a puppy.

He had chosen a spot overlooking a valley they had to cross and he scanned it now. He saw no sign of smoke or human activity. The most difficult trails were for smugglers, in the hopes that the lazy government soldiers would not be ambitious, though of course on that day Dash would have been grateful for a government patrol.

Dash thought about yesterday, about his own village. He thought about the speech he had made about not wishing to kill. He sounded like a fool in his own ears.

"Are you ready for tea?" Dash called out. "I'll take a little walk and come back. It's there, by the fire."

Dash walked ahead on the trail to get a better view of what lay ahead and to give Laila some privacy. They would avoid the valley. Altitude was better. He had no idea where the rebels had gone, but he knew that now they had prisoners, donkeys laden with stolen grain and blankets, no way could they take the high path.

When he returned, Laila had already packed, she handed him a piece of warm bread studded with almonds.

"It's only re-heated, not fresh."

"Thank you."

"Did you sleep?" she asked.

"In the mountains even the guilty sleep."

"I kept seeing Hassan the Elder's face in my dreams."

33

"I know. Let's hurry." Dash hoisted his pack and used a tree branch to brush away the remnants of their fire, so as to not leave a trail. At the edge of the clearing he looked back, only turning when he was satisfied. "You were kind to him, Laila, to all of them, yet you said nothing."

"What can you say to someone who has lost everything?" Laila sighed. "You can just breathe the same air and pray, somehow that is comforting."

"Addi, I am sorry, but you must go back to the village," Dash decided. Take them to The Oasis. Be patient with the old ones. Be careful in the Forest of Storms. Take the bridge very slowly, I don't care if it takes an hour, it saves a day of walking. Tell our elders everything."

"But I want to go on with you guys," Addi's head drooped.

"I know. I will take you on my next adventure, I promise. This is a big responsibility for you and you will earn everyone's respect."

Addi forced a smile while Laila hugged him and gave him a kiss, then they went their separate ways.

Dash and Laila walked in silence for several hours, single file, Dash set a good pace but Laila was determined to keep up.

"You can take off your headphones, Laila. I know your battery must be dead. Don't worry. I won't talk to you."

Laila gave Dash a dirty look as she removed her headphones and then stopped abruptly and pointed a finger ahead of them.

The bear was not that large, and brown, but it was still a bear. It paced for a few moments from side to side on the trail, then simply sat on its rump and yawned.

"*Asseoir avec moi, s'il vous plait*," the bear said, - then yawned again.

Dash recognized the verb "to sit" and gestured to Laila to do so. They perched on a old log a few feet away from the polite bear.

"I am Ferrous. I have been waiting for you."

"How can you talk?" Dash blurted.

"I am talking," he began, "so how does 'how' matter? " Ferrous stared at them. "I am a spirit bear," he repeated more patiently. "God made humans, and animals, and he made spirit creatures as helpers. But the humans were jealous of our powers, hunted us, and now we are very few. We keep to ourselves - you can hardly blame us." Ferrous the bear shrugged, if you can imagine a bear shrugging, and Dash nodded as if he understood.

"How did you know we would be here?" Dash wondered. "*We* didn't know we would be here."

"Dash!?" Laila turned to him. "Does it matter who knew what?" She turned back to Ferrous. "Why are you talking to us?" Laila asked in perfect French, gaining courage from the bear's melancholy demeanor. He did not seem threatening at all. "I am Laila, and the grumpy one is Dash."

"The black bird told me, of course. The one you saw at the rope bridge. Though I am a solitary creature by nature, I sometimes crave human company, as most of my own kind are gone. If you had ever to endure the limited conversational abilities of creatures of the forest, you would understand. But more importantly, I wanted to see you, Laila. The suffering of the humans is repellent to me, though I have my own grudges against your species."

"We mean you no harm, and we will tell no one of our meeting," Dash said, as he stared at Laila with new curiosity. He meant this with utter sincerity, as it had crossed his mind that no one would believe such a story anyway. He certainly couldn't tell Addi, who would never forgive him from being excluded from such an event. Bears had been extinct in the Atlas Mountains for decades. He had never heard of a sighting.

"I will show you where to cross the rapids," the bear stood now on its four legs. "And I will feed you."

Laila and Dash stared at each other. The elders had never mentioned rapids beyond the entrance to the Forest of Storms. Had he missed the trail after the village?

They walked for about ten minutes, a roaring sound getting louder. They came into a canyon. The waterfall was magnificent, and now very loud. The bear waded into the large pool and with a few deft swipes of his paw threw some fish up on a rock.

"Make your fire and cook in your manner," the bear said. "To me fire insults the flavor. I like my fish very fresh."

Laila knelt and made the fire while Dash took his knife and cleaned the fish by the water's edge.

"What is your name again, bear?" Laila asked, using the formal 'vous'. "And how may we thank you?"

"My name is called Ferrous," the bear said with great dignity.

After they had eaten their fill and talked for a long time they crossed the river on the bear's back, holding on with their legs, as the icy water roared around them. Laila held on tightly to Dash's waist.

"You must protect her, cheb," Ferrous said, using the Arabic slang for 'young man', even to the cost of your life. The people will suffer yet, but in time this child will save them and turn them to peace."

Laila scratched the bear's nose with her fingers. He groaned in pleasure.

"There is always that one spot you can never reach," he closed his eyes in delight, then spoke again. "There is a hot spring. The female will want to bathe. Sit with me while she does so."

Dash sat. The sun was warm, his stomach was full – and he was talking to a bear.

"Ferrous, you speak of the rebel God, and the true God. But how can there be more than one God, who made heaven and earth and everything in it?"

"There is God..." the bear sighed, "...and there is *Iblees*, Satan, of the Jinn. Earth is where they battle. Right now, Satan is winning."

"What is God's purpose in allowing Satan?"

"The purpose of God in allowing Satan is to forge good men in the fire. Man is separated from God, and must be purified for them to be united.

"How can I know a good man?"

"By what they do, certainly not what they say," Ferrous began. "And remember, men learn knowledge, but wisdom is from God. In particular, should you meet a leopard on the trail, be wary, for they are tricksters and can change their loyalty in a flick of their tail."

Ferrous then, without warning, fell asleep. Dash closed his eyes too, wondering if the bear was simply jealous of the leopard's fancy tail, and wondering how he, Dash, could possibly be taking a nap in the company of a bear, and finally, wondering about Laila and her bathing in the hot-spring. With these thoughts mixing like freshly ground spices, he slept.

While Dash slept, the bear awoke. He stood over Dash, opened his jaws wide, showing his teeth. He could have taken Dash's head in one bite. Instead, he lightly brushed his claw across Dash's chest, and then breathed on the bloody wound. Dash did not wake up.

When he finally awoke, the bear was gone. Laila was dressed and was brushing out her hair.

"You should bathe," she suggested. "It was wonder..." Laila gave a little shriek and stared at him, her eyes wide. "Your chest... blood!"

Dash touched his fingers to his chest. There he looked down - there were five lines, bloody but not deep, maybe six inches long.

"He marked you," Laila said in astonishment.

"I dreamed about a talking bear. We ate with him," Dash shook his head, not quite awake. "What does it mean?"

"I don't know," Laila's eyes were wide.

"We need to keep moving," Dash was not waiting for an answer.

Dash gathered their meager gear and covered the fire with dirt. He cut a leafy branch and brushed their footprints from the ground as was his habit.

"You slept for a long time," Laila said as they walked.

"I dreamed of the talking bear. It was very strange."

Laila stopped. "At first I was afraid, but he was nice. He is the reason our stomachs are full."

Dash felt his heart pounding.

"He told me to be kinder to you, that your heart was good."

"I thought you were being nice to me."

"You have no idea, Dash. You're such a boy."

"I am a year older than you. I'm almost seventeen."

Laila gave him a look that said it didn't matter, but she was amused, no longer so hostile.

They walked silently for a long time, Dash began to look for a safe place to camp for the night. Then they saw the body.

Chapter 12

The man had been dead for many years. He lay face down in a shallow wash beside their rough-hewn trail. He wore the uniform of a Moroccan soldier. The back of his shirt was stained with faded blood. Dash told Laila to stand back. He had no intention of turning the man over, but he went through his pockets looking for identification. There was some folded paper money in one pocket, denari and old francs and a faded *'carte d'identité'* that named him as Corporal Raoul Meshebe. His gun was long gone, but Dash managed to extract a dozen bullets from his belt and checked if they fit his pistol, which they did. Next he looked at the man's boots. The man was small.

"Look away," Dash unlaced the man's boots. It was grisly business but they came off. Laila's sneakers were already shredded. "At the next water I'll soak these, and as they dry they will mold to your feet."

"Not wearing dead man's boots."

"Then your feet will bleed and we will have to stop," Dash explained. "You are a girl who has never walked except to parade in your school in America and remind everyone how pretty you are."

"You have never been to my school."

"I don't need to."

"Not wearing dead man's boots."

"As you please."

Dash tied the boots together and set them down. He began gathering rocks and placing them to bury the man. There was no shortage of rocks. At first Laila just watched and then she began to help.

When they were done Dash stood up, threw the dead man's boots over his shoulder and began to walk. He had taken the dead man's identity card, his boots, his money, his bullets and his canteen. Dash had said a prayer for the man's soul. If he ever had the chance, he would pass the card to the authorities.

"I guess I am the harvester of the dead now, Laila," Dash said. "If we include your pilot and Ahmed, back on the plane, that makes three. Everyone wonders who they will become when their school is over. Now I know."

"Ahmed would have sorted us a helicopter by now and we'd be rescued and I'd be in a hot bath at a five star hotel, followed by a mani-pedi and a massage."

"Ahmed got himself killed... he your boyfriend?"

"No!" Laila snapped and then paused. "I'll admit I flirted with him. He was cool."

"What was his job?"

"He fixed... managed... things for my father."

"Your father is a bit... dramatic."

"He has a lot of responsibility. "

Dash nodded as he fingered the extra bullets in his pocket. They were in a deep canyon with high rock walls. Sound would echo, anyone listening would not be able to tell where the sound had come from.

"I need to try the gun."

"It's a gun. Don't they all work the same?"

"It's old. The bullets are old. I need to know if I can use it if we get in trouble."

That silenced her. Dash set up a rock on a larger rock and stepped back 50 paces. He planned to try one of the bullets the gun had come with, and one of the dead man's.

Click.

Click.

The bullets he had been given must have been exposed to moisture. He figured out how to take out the clip of nine, and replace the bullets with the dead man's. It took a while. He put the old bullets in his pocket, not wanting to just leave them.

Crack! The rock exploded and the sound startled both of them. Good. Dash grinned modestly. Fortune had smiled on them twice in one day. But it was wise that they kept moving.

Once out of the canyon they made camp, Laila gathered dry wood. "I miss Addi gathering the wood."

"And complaining."

They laughed. At two thousand meters of altitude the night would be very cold.

"What's a 'mani-pedi'? " Dash asked as his last thought before he drifted off to sleep."

"You can get one too, after we are rescued."

"That's not a definition," Dash whispered as he fell asleep.

Dash awoke every few hours to put wood on the fire. He could see light frost on the rocks above them. The second time he awoke he felt her back against his. It was warm. His face blushed and he quietly got up to feed the fire. They would sleep two more hours, make tea, and then move on.

Two hours later Dash was awake, but he did not move. He had been aware of rustling in the brush for some time and had slid his fingers around the gun. He would get up slowly, but be ready.

The water finally boiled.

"Shall I make two cups - or three?" Dash called out. Laila woke, confused.

The figure came out of the bushes, it was a boy younger than Dash, younger even than Addi, maybe ten, head down, with bare and bloody feet, shaking in the cold.

"Who are you?" Dash asked the boy as he stared at him. "What are you called?"

The boy did not respond, he just stared at the fire. Dash handed him tea and some left-over bread they had saved for breakfast. He devoured it, so Dash gave him his own portion also. Laila wrapped him in a blanket.

"What is your name?" She asked.

"Baz..." he looked at Dash defiantly. "And I'm not going back... anyway, there is no one left to go back to."

"What do you mean? Who is the elder there?"

The boy gave the name of Hassan, whom they had left dying. It was the village they had left that had been raided.

"You escaped?"

"I said I had to go in the bushes, then they took my shoes so that I would come back, but I didn't. I climbed the mountain instead."

"So the rebels are on the trail below us?" Dash asked. "How many are there?"

"Now?" Baz frowned. "Only three, and one of them is old. We were going too slow, with the donkeys and children, so the fighters went ahead. The ones left, they are in charge of the donkeys and supplies."

"Do they have weapons?"

The boy shrugged. Of course they had weapons.

Dash took the dead soldier's boots and handed them to Laila. "Wash his feet and then put these on him."

"Aren't those my boots?" Laila smiled. "Well, as there are only three rebels now, we can rescue the children," Laila declared. "We have the element of surprise."

"They have automatic weapons."

"You can do it, Dash," Laila said, eye-balling him.

"I thought I was a useless boy," Dash teased. "Now if Ahmed were here, we could have a helicopter and throw rocks on them from above."

"I'm sorry I said that," Laila lowered her gaze. "My father promised soldiers."

"Yes," Dash sighed as he stood up. "I would have preferred soldiers myself... Baz and I will take a look. You will wait here."

"I will *not* wait here," Laila glared.

Dash just stared at her.

"I can be the bait. A distraction."

"Bad idea."

"What if you don't come back?"

"Then go back to my village," Dash said gravely. "Tell them I am sorry, that sending me was a mistake."

Chapter 13

Baz was adept at climbing, but his face grimaced as his feet hurt inside the boots, and it took a long time. Soon enough they saw smoke from the breakfast fire. It was still early and Dash did not imagine they would expect to be attacked. After all, they were the predators.

Another hour and they were in sight of the camp. There were at least a dozen young women, girls and boys tied together with a long rope. There were also a couple of donkeys laden with blankets and bags of grain.

Two of them were younger than Dash. The other was a lot older, with a gray beard. They probably took care of supplies and cooking and had been left behind to forage. But they had good weapons.

Dash had an idea. He fingered the old bullets in his pocket. He closed his fingers around four of them and tore a piece of cloth from his clothes. He wrapped the bullets in it, tying them tightly.

"Baz," he said. "Circle around the other side of the camp and toss this into the fire. You can't miss. When they explode, I will make my move – don't get caught."

"Laila—just walk into the camp and stand by the fire - and smile."

"I'm ready for my close-up."

Baz nodded and crawled under the scrub towards the fire. Dash crouched behind some bushes and waited and watched.

Only one rebel was on guard. The other young one was handing out chunks of *khobz* to the line of prisoners. The old one was fussing with the loads on the donkeys, making sure the cinches were tight so that the loads would not slip. His weapon was leaning against a rock, and his back was to Dash. He would never get a better chance. He was not going to wait on Baz.

Laila walked to the fire and warmed her hands, as he had asked. The bearded man's head turned as he stared at her, as if at a vision.

Dash stepped out from behind the bushes and slammed the man on the back of his head with the butt of his MAC 50. As guns went, it was a terrific club. The man dropped like a stone and at that moment the bullets in the fire exploded.

Crack!

Crack!

Crack!

At least three of them did. The young rebels panicked and scampered for the scrub. The prisoners screamed and fell to the ground, sheltering their heads with their arms.

Dash grabbed the old man's automatic rifle, a Kalashnikov, and dropped to one knee, he found the safety and then aimed. He could see legs under scrub. He fired a short burst at their feet, holding it tight so the barrel wouldn't climb.

"You're surrounded!" he yelled. "Put down your weapons."

He did not have to wait long. The rebels came out with their hands in the air. They were mere boys, probably prisoners themselves a few months before. He gestured to keep their hands high. He gave Baz his knife.

"Cut the prisoners free and bring me a length of the rope."

Baz did this, as the women and boys cried and hugged each other.

Baz held the gun on the boys while Dash tied their hands behind their backs. They were sullen, heads down, their fun over.

A young mother came up to Dash. "Thank you, but what will become of us?"

"You will go back to your village and give the dead a proper burial. Baz will take you. Then you go to The Oasis. It is two, maybe three days walk, but it is downhill. My village will contact the authorities who will take these prisoners."

"We're not shooting them?" Baz interjected, disappointed.

"No, Baz, we are not shooting them... but you are promoted now to my special assistant. You and Laila help the prisoners collect their things. Make sure everyone has been fed, including these guys, and then get the donkeys turned around the other way. Make sure they have been fed too – and bring me tea! That's first."

Baz was delighted with all this responsibility. Dash grabbed the other two weapons and handed one to Laila.

"Don't shoot me."

"Don't tempt me," she said with a slow smile.

Dash kicked the old man who was coming back to consciousness and clambered to this feet, his eyes full of hate and disgust. Dash tied a hangman's noose and hung it over a sound tree branch.

"I'm going to stand you on a donkey, and then... woosh! Not bad compared to the village you visited yesterday."

"They were defiant."

Dash slammed the butt of the gun into the man's kidneys. He dropped to his knees, seared with pain.

"You mean they didn't easily surrender their wives and children? Baz! Unload a donkey. I have need of it," Dash yelled.

"You've got it, boss!"

"What do you want?" The old man snarled. "Obviously you want something."

"Where were you taking the prisoners?" Dash asked.

"To paradise."

Dash hit him again, harder.

"South of Tarfaya, on the coast, there is a camp. We go there by truck, the women who are not chosen to be wives are taken to the slave market in Laayoune. Our leaders understand that soldiers need wives and slaves, so we come and get them from the villages. The young boys are sold or put in school to learn the true path."

"Where do you meet the trucks?"

"Bou Izakam, where there are trucks which don't ask questions and few soldiers to inspect."

"Who is your leader?"

"You fool!" the old man sneered. "Our leader is your death, don't you even know? Soon enough he will be here, too late for you!"

Dash lifted the man to his feet with strange ease. He didn't yet realize the strength Ferrous the bear had given him. He walked the man over to the edge.

"What is your name?"

"Saif al Din, if you care."

"Sword of the Faith," Dash nodded. "Not bad."

"I would like time to pray," Saif al Din said stoically.

"You have time, it's a long way down."

"Who is the woman?" Saif, even facing death, stared at Laila with great interest.

"Time is short. You should contemplate your death."

The other two prisoners stared at Dash in horror. They looked like young boys now without their weapons and teenage bravado.

Dash waited several minutes, then pulled Saif al Din back from the abyss. "A canteen of water, and bread!" he yelled to Baz.

Someone handed Dash a canteen of water and a hunk of bread and a blanket. He handed them to the old man. "Go, and mutter to God as you pass."

Saif al Din eye-balled Dash. "They will kill me anyway, for losing the women."

"Who says you have to go back? Go to the medina in Fez and disappear. What obligation do you have to the devils of the mountains?

"Why are you merciful?" The old man frowned, not understanding.

"How can I ask for mercy, if I don't show it?" Dash said. Saif al Din nodded, and began to walk to the west.

The women stared at Dash in astonishment that Dash had not killed the old man, and the boys too, for that matter. Dash addressed all of them. Laila didn't say anything, but he saw judgment in her eyes.

"If I kill an old man and boys then I am no better than they are," Dash spoke, glaring at them all. "God has blessed me to be able to rescue you. You have hard days ahead. That should be your concern." Then he turned to Baz. "You are in charge – take shoes from your guards and tie their wrists. Take them to The Oasis, and show proper respect when you get there."

Dash was sorry to lose Baz, like Addi before him, but glad when the prisoners had gone. Women, girls, boys, demons and donkeys. He was used to the silence of the mountains. His thoughts too were of his own village. It had been many months since a man from the government had visited and offered protection.

The sun was high by the time they returned to their camp-site. Exhausted, he dropped the supplies he had taken from the pack mules. Just enough.

"Organize this," he said to Laila. "We can eat and then go."

"Why didn't you kill the elder?" Laila asked, not looking.

"It was not necessary."

"Then he will talk, and they will know I am in the mountains."

"He doesn't know who you are. Even I don't know who you are, and neither do you—except for some idea your father has in his head." Dash drank water and stared at her. "I promised to take you to your uncle. That's all. Anyway, I'm not ready to kill people."

"Your job is to protect me."

"The faster we move the safer you are."

They walked in silence. Maybe Laila was right, maybe he should have killed them. The burned bodies in the villages bothered Dash terribly. It was their tradition to build tombs to bury the dead, even back to the Egyptians.

Even the living sleep in tombs. When they have questions or are troubled, they would spend the night in a tomb and they would accept the answers they received in their dreams as coming from their ancestors.

But Dash did not believe that answers were so easily obtained. The ancestors now looked on with horror and had no answers for the sleepers. They stared down from the stained sky with shame at what had been done.

'Even the living sleep in tombs.' Is that great or what? Maybe that is why the pyramids are so freaking big. Maybe everybody took a sleeping bag and slept there and the dead Pharoahs would give them advice about their personal problems. That would be kind of boring if you were a dead Pharoah, though, because personal human problems are usually pretty dumb.

So, do you notice how Laila is getting a bigger part in the story now? She's not just following Dash around like a lost puppy. She is walking through the fire, literally. See the plan is – and even if you suspected it I just thought of it myself so you can't really have suspected it – I am going to finish this story by the end of detention and then I am going to give it to Laila, and when she reads it, she is going to appreciate what a great part I wrote for her. Like how a director will write a part for some actress he is all hot for, or at a minimum he thinks she can make his film a big hit, and then he'll be able to afford to get divorced and married to the actress he wrote it for in the first place.

Laila is reading. Mulch is reading also, some thick book. I glance at the clock. It's not even time for lunch.

Okay, back to our story. But we have to talk about Ferrous, is Ferrous the Bear the coolest of the cool? He kind of half mumbles, but because he is so articulate you can still understand him. And he just like falls asleep randomly, whenever. I guess when you are like about a thousand years old these things happen. Don't worry, Ferrous will be back. I mean he helped Dash, but he is really much more interested in Laila. I can respect that. Whatever Laila is reading, she'll like this better.

Chapter 14

They each walked with a blanket under their backpacks, as they had for the past two days, always climbing the narrow path.

Laila had shown Dash how to cut a slit in each blanket for their heads to go through, which did not compromise the effectiveness of the blanket at night.

"The Mexicans invented it, so they could keep their hands free to reach for their 'pistolero'," Laila giggled.

"And you were in America how long? Three years?" Dash grinned, "And you learned to reach for a 'pistolero'?

Laila stooped and picked up a stone, and threw it at him. "I saw it in a cowboy movie - and just for the record - I've never touched a man's 'pistolero'."

"So America was not that much fun, then?"

Dash ducked as another stone flew by his head and he picked up the pace.

"Have you ever seen a movie, Dash?"

Water was now a problem, so they kept their eyes on the rocks above for tiny rivulets that would begin when the snow melted as the day warmed, gathering it in their canteens when they could, and stopping to drink their fill and make tea.

Wood was a challenge too, so they gathered it where they could. And Laila's shoes... Dash had wrapped laces around her left one where the sole had separated. Now what was this buzzing sound?

Laila spotted it first. A white hovering circle. "It's called a drone. It probably has a camera. In America kids have them - and the military."

"How big is it?" Dash frowned, shading his eyes. "How far away?"

"I don't know. Someone is spying on us."

"They can use that to watch us?"

"Yes, to see where we are, and then send fighters to wait for us along the trail." Laila's tone was grave.

Dash dropped to his knees, shrugged off his back pack, and shouldered the newest looking of the weapons they had taken.

"Where should I hit it?"

"In the middle?" Laila had no idea but wanted to help. "That must be where the battery is. The battery would be the heaviest part, so they would have to put it in the middle, don't you think?"

Dash had no idea, but he had shot many game birds. He knew how to lead and shoot between heartbeats, but this drone just hovered, arrogantly. In fact it was moving closer. Dash slowed his breathing and waited.

"Crack, crack, crack," he let off a burst. The AK slammed hard into his shoulder and the barrel climbed. He hit nothing. Try again.

"Crack, crack, crack." The sound echoed off the mountain walls which for centuries had known nothing but silence.

"Crack, crack, crack." Chunks of white plastic flew off the body of the drone.

"Crack, crack, crack." Dash finished the clip and waited. Yes. Smoke. The drone spun in lazy circles as whoever was flying it from a computer screen tried to get it back under control. Dash slammed in another clip.

"Crack, crack, crack." The drone came towards them now, faster and faster, faster than they could imagine. Dash threw down the AK and threw his body over Laila, knocking her into the stony ground as the drone crashed into the mountain above them and pieces of plastic and rock rained down.

"You hurt me."

"That's my job."

Dash jumped up and began climbing, ignoring Laila's complaints. He wanted to see this thing. It had crashed into a crevice.

As the dust and clattering of small rocks stopped, Dash and Laila stared at the white, tail-less fuselage sticking out of the side of the mountain just above them. Their ears rang from the echoes.

How can it be stuck in a mountain? Dash wondered. He shouldered his rifle and began to climb over the rocks to check it out.

"No! It's too dangerous," Laila yelled.

Dash looked back, "Not anymore!" he laughed.

Laila was covered with fine dust. He imagined that he was too. For a moment he felt sorry for her. She would be much happier in America.

Dash tried to rock the fuselage from side to side, it was not heavy, and not as big as he had feared. He had been lucky to hit it.

"Help me," he yelled. "We have to throw it over the edge."

"Why? Laila sounded annoyed.

"Because they might come looking for it," Dash was panting from his climb. "I don't know what kind of range these have, but fighters are down below us somewhere."

"Be careful!"

Laila climbed up to help, and they managed to break off a large chunk of the wreck. Inside were various cables and wires, there was the harsh smell of burnt chemicals and fried electricity. A bullet had gone right through one of the batteries and the chemicals had splattered on the plastic fuselage and on the rocks.

Dash thought of looking through it for anything that might be useful, but there was no time. The crash would have been heard for miles, and Dash knew that the rebels would not waste this sort of weapon on some useless girl.

He hefted the wreckage off the side of the mountain. He couldn't see where it landed, but it made impressive sounds.

"I think there is water up there, where it crashed."

They climbed back up into the narrow crevice, by turning sideways Dash could get through and it widened again. One wall of sheer rock was wet with snow water.

"Yes! Pass me your canteen."

Dash filled Laila's canteen and then his own, and then drank his fill. He walked deeper into the crevice and went around a corner.

"There's a cave! Laila, let's get our things!"

"I thought we had to keep moving?"

"We can stay here tonight. If they can track the wreckage they'll go down below into the canyons, away from us."

The cave was huge, and they couldn't see where it ended. There was a small fire pit inside, and ancient wood that would burn too fast, but at least it would burn. It seemed no one had been there for many years. Water, wood and shelter. Paradise.

Dash scrounged more wood then boiled water while Laila organized their food, then found large flat rocks that would reflect heat. Tonight would be the coldest yet.

"So who is going to sleep in the middle?" Laila teased. "With Addi and Baz gone?"

"I will pile rocks between us," Dash said. "As tall as the sky."

Okay. This is what happens in life. Finally I get Dash and Laila alone in the cave with time to kill. No, it's not the Four Seasons, but it's not worse than Robert Jordan and Maria in a sleeping bag under a Spanish sky.

Dash definitely likes Laila, even if she makes him crazy, and she is starting to like him. I mean I hope she's not going to friend-zone him, do you? Anyway there is LOTS of potential here. No one will ever know what is going to happen in the cave tonight, and then 'Wham!' Out of nowhere... man I never saw this coming.

It happened without warning. Dash rolled on the ground in agony, clutching at his calf. "Hayya!!" Laila shrieked the Arabic word for 'snake', as one slithered between some dark rocks. It was about half a meter long. Dash's heart pounded, his head was throbbing and he was too dizzy to stand. He had a strange roaring in his ears. So this is how it ends? He had heard the stories from the village elders while sitting around the fire and now he was terrified.

It would take time, but soon enough his heart and lungs would be paralyzed and he would die of respiratory failure. Laila knelt beside him now, sobbing.

"I'm sorry, Laila," Dash gasped. I should have known better than to explore in here. Snakes love dark caves. Can I have some water, please?"

Laila brought him water, she said something but he couldn't hear her because of the roaring in his ears.

"Dash, you won't die, Dash!" said a voice in Dash's head. "I had to bite you to give you a gift."

Dash sat bolt upright so fast Laila fell backwards and just stared. Dash's eyes turned to the snake, now coiled on a higher rock, its head in the air, it's hood extended, its eyes large and round. It was black except for a creamy mottled belly, the tongue flicking in and out. But it was the eyes that held you, the head cocked to one side like a curious puppy.

"Dash, you have to breathe," the voice spoke again. "You have to lower your heart rate or you will have a problem."

Dash tried to breathe, and slowly he calmed down. It would never had been possible to calm himself had they not already experienced Ferrous the bear.

"Laila," Dash spoke her name without breaking gaze with the snake. "This is a spirit animal, like Ferrous... I won't die... unless she is lying to me."

"It's a female?" Laila showed new interest.

"I don't know, that's just what's in my head. I can understand what she says."

"Ferrous helped us..."

"I know. She says it is safe to stay here. Explore the cave. There is a hot spring in the back. Take the green moss from the rocks in the water and put it on my wound. She said I will have some of her powers, but I must be careful not to bleed. If I bleed too much, I will diminish my powers. I will sleep. In the morning I will know what to do. She says it is easier for her to talk to me in my dreams. My brain is too noisy and I am giving her a headache."

Dash almost laughed but instead snorted and coughed. Laila held his head and gave him some more water. She was about to speak, but she saw that Dash was already asleep, he had a slight fever. She waited beside him and saw that his chest was moving evenly. She folded his blanket and put it under his head. She found a suitable stick outside and made a torch from their small supply of pitch to explore the cave. The snake had disappeared.

Laila walked through an archway, in fact she had to bend her head to do so, then she was in a huge cavern with magnificent pictures carved and painted on the stone walls, the pictures were perhaps twenty feet tall.

She knew they were petroglyphs, only these looked almost Egyptian. More sophisticated than those at Tassili n'Ajjer, which anyway were much older. The lines were black from iron and manganese particles having oxidized over hundreds of years and interacting with minute organic matter and dust. One image was rays from a golden sun, there were large images of people, maybe two or three meters tall, some with animal heads that looked like they were decorated with real gold. She wished her iPhone was charged, or any camera, because no one would believe what they had discovered, especially this far west. Tassili n'Ajjer was far across the Sahara. This was different.

The main image was a queen or princess on a chair, or litter, being carried by slaves, a black cobra coiled around her arm and looking at her, as though they were having a conversation. Dihya. The long train of people and animals meant that she was on a journey.

She realized it was true. Dihya. The warrior queen. A shiver ran up her spine. Why had the snake not bitten her instead of Dash?

As Laila walked further into the cavern, she heard the sound of water trickling, there was water coming down the wall, and a small stream that trickled into a steaming pond that disappeared under some rocks on the other side. The water was hot. She took Dash's knife and scraped the moss from the rocks as Dash had said, then cupped her hands and drank and felt invigorated.

She went back to Dash and found the two small puncture wounds and covered them with the moss.

Then she went outside the cave and stared to the west as the sun set. There were low clouds. Perhaps beyond them they could see the ocean. Her uncle Taha. Perhaps in the morning they could see all the way to the ocean, and they would know what they must do. She imagined the descent must begin soon. How did the snake survive at this cold altitude? She guessed a spirit snake didn't have to worry about things like that.

Laila saw that Dash was in a deep sleep. He did not seem to be in pain. She tended the fire, then used almost the last of their starter and flour to make some taguella that she could bake on the rocks in the morning. It was Dash's favorite and he was always hungry. She changed the moss on his wound while he moaned in his sleep. The she wrapped her own blanket around her shoulders and ate some almonds and dried figs, and drank hot mint tea and stared at Dash's face in the firelight. He was a beautiful boy when he wasn't bossing her around. It was her fine intention to stay awake and watch over him, but the utter silence of the ancient cave and the soft crackle of the fire soon enough lulled her to sleep.

She never knew that the snake joined them near the fire, to enjoy the warmth, to talk to Dash in his dreams, and to stare at Laila with great curiosity.

Dash was awake early and had replenished the fire and tea.

"Thank you," Laila said. "I was going to get up before you and make bread."

"It's not too late," Dash smiled. "I saw the walls. That queen that is being carried on a litter, with the snakes, she looks just like you! You could be twins. She must be the warrior queen you were talking about."

"Dihya Kahina - the warrior queen - Dash, she's been dead for fourteen hundred years!"

"She could still look like you from back then. Why didn't the snake bite you? You're the chosen one."

"I don't know, I was wondering the same thing." Laila said. "I could live with being less chosen."

"How old are the drawings?"

"They would have to do tests, the dry air will have protected them. Was the snake in your dreams?"

"She has taken the name Cleo, from her friend the Egyptian, Cleopatra."

"That was a thousand years ago!"

"God's time is not our time. Cleo was a spirit animal, an advisor, to Cleopatra, is what she told me. She is giving me a gift through her venom in my blood and help us. And she told me that the rebels have decided to wait for us at the bottom of the mountain."

"So it was a mistake to not kill the old man."

"I told you, I'm not ready to kill people," Dash glared.

"We should stay here for a few hours. Bathe and rest. You saw the hot spring."

Dash's first instinct was to say no. They had to stay in motion, but... if he were exhausted than Laila must be too.

"Okay. Do you want to bathe first?"

Dash stared into the fire while Laila went off to the hot spring. He hadn't said a word to her, but the cave paintings had freaked him out more than the snake. What the heck was going on? Who was Laila, really? And how was he supposed to protect her? With those troubling thoughts he dosed off. Laila came back an hour later carrying her washed clothes, wearing just the blanket. She spread them on the flats rocks outside in the sun. Then she lay down with her head on Dash's stomach and tried to sleep too.

She had done as her father had asked. She had promised him everything. But she wanted her own life. Being free with Dash, this adventure, even with the danger... it beat sitting in math.

Seeing her likeness painted on the wall of a cave in the Atlas mountains from forever ago... what was up with that? She imagined sitting in a cafe with her friends and trying to explain this thing that was happening. How?

Dihya had slit a King's throat to free her people. What were her uncle and father plotting that they hadn't felt it necessary to tell her?

She listened to Dash's heart beating. Strong, even breathing. She ran her fingers over the scabs of blood on his chest where Ferrous the Bear had marked him. It was healing. No infection. Dash gave a snort and his body twitched in his sleep. What was Cleo telling him?

Laila got dressed. The moment passed. They had to be serious and not complicate things.

An hour later Dash woke up and went to bathe. Laila found a small rough-surfaced stone and tried to fix her broken nails.

They ate and packed their things without much talk, both lost in thought. Dash's face went pale.

"Are you okay?"

"Cleo... says we should rest here another night."

"What do you think?"

"I am concerned about our food... at this altitude..." Dash shook his head and then his face twitched. "Okay!" he shouted. Laila just stared.

"She is bossy!" Dash laughed a bit weirdly. "There are partridge nearby. If we clean them and bury them in the coals the feathers come off easily. Take the mud from the hot spring and cover them in it."

"She's teaching you how to cook?"

"Apparently."

"I don't think Cleopatra of Egypt cooked much."

"Scrounge firewood, I'll get the food." Dash checked his weapon.

That night they lay by their fire. Some of the wood was green, so it snapped and popped. Their stomachs were full. Dash had placed more flat stones to radiate heat.

"It's snowing!" Laila jumped up and wrapped her blanket around her shoulders. Let's go see."

Outside random snowflakes danced. Laila clapped her hands in delight and tried to catch one. Dash looked scared of them and she laughed even harder. "Try and catch one on your tongue!"

"Maybe this is why Cleo wanted us to stay, so we'd have shelter tonight." They were standing very close together.

"Look!" Dash pointed up at the brilliant stars. "That is Alnilam - it means 'string of pearls' - Orion's belt – not that I'd know a pearl."

"What else don't you know?" Laila leaned forward and kissed him.

I spent a lot of time on the cave drawings . I finished some shading on the drawing of the partridge roasting over their fire, the light flickering on the cave walls. It looks pretty good, actually. Then, snowflakes outside? If this isn't romantic I don't know what it's going to take. I guess you can't put some vintage R&B on the turntable and ask her to dance anymore than I can right here in detention. Crap. Laila wore high heels to detention. Stilettos. This girl is too much. Enjoy your moment with Laila, Dash, because you should have killed Saif, the Sword of Faith guy when you had the chance. He's going to be nothing but grief now.

Chapter 15

"There is their camp," Laila had spotted it. They crouched behind some rocks and scrub and scanned the valley floor. It was early on the fourth day since they'd left the safety of the cave.

Two tents, an awning, two battered pick-up trucks—and a couple of dirt bikes. One pick-up looked like it was loaded with other tents and gear.

"No one... not even a guard," said Laila, "Looks like they are moving out?"

"They would have good sight lines from above us. Maybe their plan is to watch the valley floor and then run us down when we are out in the open."

"Then we should cross at night," Laila said.

Dash looked around, preoccupied, restless teenage energy bubbling... until he spotted an impressive mass of boulders between them and the camp.

"I'm going to try and start a rock slide. You watch. That may force them into the open."

"Then what? What happened to crossing at night?"

"Wait here."

Dash climbed, trying to be quiet, maybe up five hundred meters, It was harder than it looked. He got his shoulder under a large bolder that looked tip-able. Normally he could not have moved it an inch, but he wanted to feel what Ferrous the bear had given him.

He leaned into the rock, it slid a fraction, but then excitedly released. Gravity took over and a dozen or more rocks tumbled, making an powerful noise, and also raising a lot of dust.

He looked down at Laila, wanting her approval of his impressive commotion. She rewarded him with a thumbs down and then, at last, a smile.

He ran back down to join her. "They didn't sleep through that."

"Maybe they underestimated our speed coming down. And they are up in the mountains behind us."

Dash didn't like this idea.

"What if you disable their vehicles, and we take off? They would not be able to catch us on foot.

"Let's go down and take a look," Dash decided. "It looks like a trap... but... what choice do we have?"

Dash put his weapon off safety. "Can you ride a dirt bike?"

"Do you think I can't?" Laila growled, thinking that this was all about the motor bikes, not escaping, but escaping pulling wheelies in a cloud of dust. "You're such a boy!" Laila yelled down at him.

I warned Dash the boulder thing was a truly bad idea. But I super enjoyed drawing it, flying rocks and dust and debris. I sharpened my pencil. Anyway, Dash has had it way too easy. Having cave-time with Laila while I am stuck here in detention? I'm not forgetting that. Time for Dash to suffer.

Chapter 16

Laila and Dash were about fifty meters from the dirt bikes and saw no one. Maybe someone in the tent?

Still nothing. Dash hated this plan, but the motorcycles were close. Nothing. Dash kicked the dirt, looking for a hidden chain or other trick. He touched the engines. Cold.

"Let's go!" He ordered hoarsely. He started the engine for Laila and pointed to the easiest path, a gap between two hills to the west. "Go!" He revved the engine and took off.

Laila was doing all right, Dash thought. Her head down, heading straight to the gap. They sped through the scrub and sand. To the south was the real desert, the Sahara, to the north another wall of mountains.

Then they were going up hill, swerving between the endless scrub and boulders. Once they were over the crest they might be able to spot a dirt road or path.

Laila's engine died first. The rattling gasp of no petrol. She turned and looked at Dash, who stopped.

"Leave it! Get on." Laila dropped the bike and climbed on behind Dash. He motioned for her to hold on. The crest was just ahead. He wanted to look for a road before dark.

They didn't hear the explosion, just the shock wave and the rain of stone and dirt and the sound of their own coughing.

Dash staggered to his feet and peered through dust. At that moment Dash's engine died too. The echo of the explosion faded, the dust began to clear.

"Put down your weapons."

There were two men, one barely older than Dash. Then there was the old man, Saif al Din. The 'Sword of Faith' whom Dash had spared after the village massacre.

"Shock grenade," Saif admitted. "Expensive, but I could not risk injuring our prize."

Laila shook her head at Dash. Behind her, Dash could see four more thuggish men coming over the crest from the west. Not kids, real fighters. He looked at Laila with shame in his eyes. He remembered his promise to her father and wandered his hand towards the trigger as he knelt to place it on the ground.

Saif was looking back at the returning fighters, he had time to kill Saif and maybe one or two others, but the odds were bad, there was no shelter. Or he could just shoot Laila.

He did not look at Laila. He couldn't. Not after the second night in the cave. There would be a way to escape. Have faith.

"Half a litre of petrol," Saif al Din announced. "Just enough to strand you in open ground. I am old, I cannot chase you, so I had to lay a good trap."

Dash's face burned with shame. How stupid had he been?

One of the returning fighters walked straight up to Laila and slapped her face.

"Cover yourself!"

As he raised his hand to strike her again Laila grabbed his wrist and twisted him to his knees.

Saif al Din lazily fired a shot in the air, and everyone froze. The thug rose and reluctantly moved away from Laila.

"I'm doing it!" Laila rooted in her back-pack for a scarf as the other men laughed.

"These are all we have to sell at Laayoune?" Someone challenged Saif. "You lost the others?"

"The girl... will bring a great price—if she is untouched."

"Then let us have the unshaven boy for our pleasure. He looks like a girl anyway," the man sneered and jutted his jaw towards Dash. "We have been in these mountains too long."

Saif looked like he was considering the idea. "It is only one day's drive to the market. So you can wait for your reward—these prisoners are not to be touched. Put some petrol in the bikes. We will strike camp in the morning."

It was night by the time they walked back across the valley floor to the encampment. Dash's mood was black with shame and disgust that he had been tricked. But at least they had time to escape before they reached Laayoune.

But then he and Laila were separated. He had not been expecting that. Dash was tied to a scrubby tree with very good knots and given a few gulps of water. Plenty of time to contemplate his screw-up.

The night was long and cold and the knots were tight. In the morning two fighters prodded Laila to climb into the back of the pick-up. Saif walked over to Dash and dropped Dash's backpack, one blanket, a bottle of water and a chunk of bread. "My obligation to you is satisfied. If we meet again you will not be spared."

Saif turned to his men. "Let's go! It's a long drive to paradise."

It took hours for Dash to free himself. He walked back across the scrub and over the crest where the motor bikes had died. Yes, he could see a dirt road. It followed the edge of the scrub and sand. Walking across the sand would save him many hours, but he knew that only a fool would do that without supplies.

Then he saw the lines in the sand. They were moving, slithering, like snakes, but there were no snakes. He stepped forward, and new lines formed ahead of him. It was path. How was this happening?

He walked forward, new lines formed. He looked behind him. Nothing. He disappeared into the desert. He knew he had to keep the afternoon sun on his right to be heading south. Beyond that there was no navigation. 'Sand remembers nothing' was an expression of the nomads of the desert. Each wind paints a new picture, Dash knew this since he was a child.

Hours later it was dark and cold. He wrapped himself in his blanket, stared up at the brilliant stars and fell into a fitful sleep, thinking of how frightened Laila must be.

In the morning the snake lines were there again, and he kept walking. It took all day to reach some substantial scrub, but another hour brought him to a dirt road, where he saw a dust cloud behind him. It was a Volkswagen mini-van, with a roof rack loaded with luggage.

"How do you speak English so well?" The curly-blond haired American man who was driving asked over his shoulder.

"I was bitten by a snake," Dash said absently, a bit loopy from his ordeal "...and then I could understand."

"In America, 'snake-bit' is what you call someone who has very bad luck," the other American, a woman, added.

"That sounds about right," Dash said. "I am Dash Lahlou, and I am grateful that you found me and are giving me a ride."

"I'm Dave and this is Dixie. We are journalists, we travel around and do stories for American magazines and radio. Dixie here takes amazing pictures. She's been in National Geographic."

"Are you a Berber?" Dixie asked. She had long dark hair cut in bangs, and glasses. But her face was too old for the bangs and she was a bit fat, Dash thought. But she had given him a bottle of water.

"My family has lived in The Oasis for as long as anyone can remember. It is in the mountains on the Algerian and Moroccan border. Everyone is welcome there, even in war. We do not differentiate people by their place or their color, only by their nature, whether good or evil... to where is this car going?" Dash squinted as he looked out the window.

"We are going to the United Nations refugee camp south of Laayoune to check out a story for NPR."

Dave lit a joint and passed it back to Dash, who did not smoke, but for today he felt obligated to his rescuers and inhaled, then passed the joint back to Dixie. "The light is so good right now Dave. Let's shoot him on those rocks up ahead."

Dash's eyes widened. "Shoot me?"

"With this, she laughed, reaching down into a canvas bag and pulling out a 35mm camera.

They pulled over to the side of the road. Dash climbed up on the rocks and squinted into the golden sun. He felt a bit dizzy from the joint, but he smiled and did what Daisy wanted.

"The camera loves him!" Daisy exclaimed as she clicked away.

"The slave market will love him," Dave muttered.

Daisy scrolled through images showing Dash his pictures, and other people they had shot.

"Who is that?" Dash asked sharply as he saw a very good picture of a silver-bearded older man with fierce eyes.

"Saif?" Dave said. He's our amigo, he runs a mining operation at the volcano on the Atlantic coast. They call it The Holy Mountain.

"Mining?" Dash frowned. "What sort of mining?"

"No idea. The true believers," Dave began, "think the mountain keeps a Jinn, a demon, pinned under it, guarded by terrifying scorpions, and they believe the demon will be grateful to be released."

"We have never seen such scorpions," Daisy admonished. "It is forbidden."

"Regular scorpions are bad enough - do you have a pocket knife?" Dash asked. Dave reached into his pocket, handed Dash the knife and watched as he cut open the waist band of his ragged pants and extracted the jewels his grandmother had given him. He handed them to Daisy.

"Take me there. To this Holy Mountain."

"He's asleep again." Daisy said to Dave as she stared at Dash in the back seat.

"Good, makes it easy," Dave answered.

"The mine will give us a better price than the slave market for him."

Dash's eyes were slits.

"Let's keep him tonight." Daisy said with enthusiasm. "We can sell him just as well tomorrow."

Dave's expression darkened.

"I'll let you watch, this time," Dixie said.

"He's pretty stoned. I don't think he smokes."

"That will make it easier."

"I don't think so. What if he escapes?"

"I'll let you take pictures. He's beautiful."

"Drug him. Mushrooms. The good ones."

"Of course."

Chapter 17

Dash heard voices, yelling. He drained a bottle of water and squinted over the dashboard. A rebel fighter was yelling into a walkie-talkie. Something about money. He gestured at Dave and Dixie. It was a guard post, there was a large-ish tent a few meters off the road. In the distance he saw some single-story gray industrial looking buildings clustered around this end of an ancient volcano. It wasn't impressive, if you were expecting a holy mountain, Dash thought.

Then two other men casually came over to the mini-van and gestured for him to get out.

"Look up and smile," the head thug said.

Dash heard a whirring sound and looked up at the sky. A small drone hovered above them, and then zoomed away.

More talking. Daisy kept glancing back at Dash as she spoke. Dash did not look at her. What she had done to him last night had been disgusting but he had been too stoned to resist. Now he was ashamed and didn't want to think about it.

Then the head thug turned his back on them and disappeared into the tent.

He came out carrying a thick wad of money, which he handed to Dave, who busily counted it, and then handed it to Daisy who stuffed it in her bag. The thug then walked over to Dash, eyeing him, and spoke in Arabic.

"I am Raoul."

"I am Dash."

"Dash, you understand that your friends have just sold you, to me, like a lump of meat?"

"They are not my friends. I paid them to bring me here."

"No one has ever done that, except true believers who come to join us."

"What I believe is not so clear right now, but I am very interested in your mountain."

"So I did not need to pay for you?"

"You should save your money for the trouble ahead, Raoul. I told you, I paid to come here."

Dave and Daisy walked past Dash and Raoul, staring at the dirt. Dash's eyes followed them. The thug then pulled a pistol from his belt and handed it to Dash. "You are young, to say such things as you speak. I am curious to see what you will do."

Dash took off the safety and chambered a round, knowing well that one false move and the weapon trained on him would fire. He nodded to Raoul as he walked around to the driver's side and put the gun to Dave's head.

"Return the money or return the jewels. I paid already for the ride, it is enough."

"Sure... sure," Dave sweated. "Just be careful with that gun, kid."

"What?" Daisy shrieked "The hell we will," as she foraged in her voluminous hand bag.

Dash now aimed the gun at Daisy's head. "Give me the gun, and the cash, very slowly."

Daisy did that with an evil sneer, then Dash handed Raoul the thick wad of his cash and both guns.

They watched as Dave managed a three point turn and drove away in a cloud of dust. A few hundred feet down the road the mini-van stopped, and there was a single gun shot. Then the passenger door opened, and the body of Daisy rolled out into the dirt.

"I guess he was sick of her, too."

Dash gazed at the volcano, then at the ocean beyond. It sparkled in the light. He had never seen it.

"How old are you?"

"Sixteen."

"We will start you in the mine, then you will be questioned again. That will test anyone's faith," Raoul laughed and patted Dash on the shoulder.

"What do you mine?" Dash asked.

"We mine faith. With God's blessing you will find it."

"Okay."

"Hey!" Raoul yelled back towards the guard tent. "Release a scorpion to get the body. Our friends will feast tonight."

Dash stared as a huge scorpion, at least 4 feet long, on a long chain held by a man with a long black beard marched toward Daisy's body.

This was going to be disgusting.

"Oh, I waited for this! I have been drawing scorpions all morning. Now I'm going to draw the scorpion dragging Daisy's body back to its lair. If that doesn't scare the crap out of Dash nothing will. And The Holy Mountain is so anticlimactic, just a tapped out volcano full of rocks and dust. Demon my ass. But Dash is such a country boy he has no clue. So Laila is a prisoner of the rebels, in their Holy Mountain. Do they even understand who she is? Is Dash going to be able to manage this? I had better figure out how to rescue Laila!

Chapter 18

The ancient face was crossed with lines like dry river beds. He managed a warehouse-sized cave with wooden shelves of blankets, clothing and equipment. Dash was given two blankets, two sets of work clothes, a water bottle, and new sandals.

"Trade with each other for size," the ancient one said as he directed him to another table where he was given some bread, not skillfully made, and water and fruit. It mattered not, he was starving. He ate, found an empty cot, and slept until dawn.

The next morning his name was called. As a volunteer, he was given charge of half a dozen men who seemed to have nothing in common except basic Arabic and bad luck.

The equipment was ancient, as was the methodology. They were escorted to the entrance to a rock face at dawn. A blast crew would emerge from the corridor carrying drills and dynamite. Then there would be a 'thump' and an impressive cloud of smoke and heat would emerge into the common tunnels. The more experienced men wore wet bandanas over their faces until the blasting was over. There were two phases to the work. First to clean out all the blasted rock and load it into rolling carts which were taken away and returned empty. Late in the day a man would come and inspect the tunnel. If deemed necessary, wood and and tools would be brought and they would build some rudimentary framing to prevent cave-ins. They worked by lantern light.

After twelve hours they were taken to another communal cave where they bathed under a large waterfall from an underground spring. This was the fresh water supply for the entire mountain. There was neither soap nor towels.

"Where does it go?" Dash asked one of the regular guards, who just shrugged.

"To the ocean, I guess. No one has ever come back to tell us."

"Some have tried to escape?"

"All are welcome to try. We don't even waste bullets on them."

"Where do they keep the women?"

"Questions and death are close companions here, brother."

"Sure. Just curious."

Food was always grilled fish and some boiled grain, sometimes fruit, twice a day. It was never enough.

If the team made their quota of rock, they were given a packet of qat, an east African plant that gave a mild high when chewed, and also helped to kill the appetite. Some men would trade, thinking if they were going to be hungry anyway they may as well be stoned.

On the 3rd day Dash volunteered to take the cart full of rock to be dumped. No one volunteered for this job, but he was the strongest, and he hoped he could learn the tunnels and different parts of the mountain. But by the 5th day he was still getting nowhere learning about where the women were kept.

On the 6th day they did not work. Tonight would be a special event. Dash spent the day laying on his back, away from the others, trying to think. Wishing Cleo would tell him something. This work was getting him nowhere.

A man slightly cleaner and slightly more dignified in bearing than most, his beard still black, brought him food. This was unusual.

"I am Yusef. Tell me, cheb, what have you learned since you have been here?"

"That hunger will always be my companion."

"Then you hunger for the wrong things."

"I don't choose to be hungry. I am hungry because I labor, and my body needs food to be able to labor."

"I will repeat myself, you have hunger for the wrong things."

"I told God I was hungry. He laughed at me."

"You must make your prayers with respect. Prayer is not asking for things."

"Does God laugh at you?"

"No, because I have faith."

"How does one acquire faith?"

"Make your prayers with respect. Be thankful for one bowl of grain, not sad because you do not have two."

"I kind of agree with that, but we travel in a circle, because I am required to work, yet my body needs food. If you show a man a tree, and tell him it must be cut down, yet you do not give him an axe, is it reasonable of you to expect him to cut the tree with faith alone?"

"You do not ask the questions a man searching for faith would ask," the man frowned as he stood. "So I do not believe your sincere purpose in being here... nor do I care what your true purpose is... however, you have been an excellent worker, and I will permit you another chance to stay on this side of death. Tonight there will be an event for the amusement of the workers. You will have an opportunity to commit an act of faith. So get some sleep. Someone will come for you in due course. I tell you honestly to prepare yourself, because very few pass this test. Perhaps your faith can be found in a significant death."

On that cheerful note the man Yusef left and Dash finished his food.

Let me finish drawing the tail on this fellow. 'Dash versus the Giant Scorpion?' Maybe I'll call the story that, but it might not impress Laila. Maybe 'Dash Battles the Giant Scorpion for Laila's Honor? Never mind. We'll work on the title later. Let's get to the good part. Dash has to rescue Laila, but first he has to defeat these foul creatures. Of course I created them, so I guess I could have made them less foul, but what fun would that have been? Laila is locked in a shipping crate, and let out only twice a day. Does she have any confidence that Dash will show up? After all it's been a couple of days now...

Chapter 19

Dash gazed about the huge cavern known as The Pit, one of many that veined the mountain. Slaves must have built the crude wooden bleachers, like a budget coliseum.

Half a dozen sharpened wooden spears and a wooden shield. What a joke when the guards had AKs. The crowd filed in, pausing to look into the cage where the lucky contestants crouched, wild-eyed and fearful.

As the spectators entered they each took a wooden torch and dipped it into one of the huge vats of tar which were placed at various points around the stadium, then set it aflame. These would be waved around during the contest to provide both light and atmosphere. There was no electricity in this part of the mountain, though they had seen natural tar pits outside. The spectators also chewed an East African leaf known as khat, a stimulant chewed the way some Americans used chewing tobacco.

The crowd placed bets. Giant scorpions, like the one he had seen sent to eat Daisy, were chained to the stone walls and then released for each match. Two scorpions against one human, sometimes two humans against four or more of creatures. The humans rarely won. The bets were mostly on who would be the last to die. The weapons provided were worse than those of Roman times.

The next two scorpions came out of the tunnel hesitantly. They were huge, at least 3 or 4 feet long not counting the lobster-like pincers. Blue, with reddish claws, though that may have been dry blood. They had a hesitant, almost sideways scurrying motion, but no mistake, they were fast. The contestant didn't last thirty seconds, and after lifting the body up in the air on its tail in victory the winning scorpion dragged it back into the tunnel to feast. The crowed booed disappointment at the pitiful performance of the human.

And so it went. Dash studied their behavior, trying to see if they cooperated with each other and if they had any weaknesses. He wasn't sure if they even had eyes, then he remembered that they hunted by sensing vibrations in the ground. If he could stand still perhaps he would be 'invisible' and the vibrations from the crowd might confuse it and he would have a chance.

Then it was time. He was the final contestant. He rubbed sand on his palms to make sure he would have a good grip.

A man with a battery-powered megaphone took his elbow and announced Dash to the crowd. Dash pumped his arm in the air. He wanted the crowd on his side.

Next, a man was dragged out and thrown on the dirt in front of Dash, his hands chained behind him. It was not a man Dash knew, just someone he recognized from seeing in the tunnels.

The announcer handed Dash a sword and explained the next event to the crowd, who didn't seem that interested.

"If you execute the prisoner, you are excused from having to fight the scorpion."

The crowd booed .

"If you spare the prisoner, you have to fight the scorpion."

"I get to think this over, right?"

"Sure, for ten or fifteen seconds."

The crowd roared with a bit more enthusiasm, Dash again pumped his arm in the air and took the sword in his other hand. They wanted him to fight the scorpion. The prisoner was dragged away, he frowned. He did not understand why Dash had spared him. Dash threw the sword on the ground and the crowd went crazy.

Laila sat in a small wooden cage, a shipping crate. Her wrists were tied with rope and her shoes gone. She worked on the knot with her teeth. No one had said anything to her. She could not see much in the dim light but could hear weeping and moaning all around. She had seen several young women being taken into another cavern, she didn't know to what purpose. Only that it would be bad.

Then she saw it. A nail not properly countersunk in the wood, sticking out perhaps a 1/4". It was enough. She twisted her body so she could rub the rope against the head of the nail.

The crowd roared as the guard unlocked Dash's ankle chains. This time just one scorpion came out of the tunnel, but it was the largest yet, at least six feet long including the tail. Dash could see the flaming torches waving drunkenly in the crowd. He edged close to one of the tar vats and dipped his spear into it, then lit the spear on a spectator's torch. A flaming spear. No one had tried this, the crowd murmered to each other. They were happy to help him, the entertainment had been thin tonight.

Dismissing his plan of standing still, he did not hesitate. The crowd roared in delight as Dash ran between the grasping claws of the creature, like a boxer getting inside his opponent's long reach. The thing smelled disgusting. Dash could see the poison tail arching. He had one chance to get a solid plant. He shoved the flaming spear into where the creature's throat should be but did not let go. Instead he bent his knees and lifted the scorpion into the air, using his bear-given strength to heave the creature back into the vat of pitch, then throwing himself face down into the dirt. When the pitch met the flame it exploded, covering hundreds of the spectators with burning oil, poison and scorpion guts.

Dash screamed as his back was splattered with burning tar, but then he jumped up and ran into the entrance tunnel he had been brought to, reaching down to grab the sword off the floor.

A guard who had been distracted staring at the disaster tried to unhook his weapon from his shoulder, but he was too slow as Dash impaled his thigh. Dash grabbed his assault rifle and then his side-arm, stuffing it in his pants. He threw away the sword and then knelt down and fired a low burst into the dirt on the floor of the tunnel behind him. That should slow things down.

And he ran as best he could in cheap sandals. He had to find Laila.

An old man came and unlocked Laila's cage.

"Water," she pleaded in Arabic, trying to look weak, her hands pressed against her stomach. The man dragged her out and gestured for her to follow him. She staggered and bumped against him, then fell to one knee. He snarled "walk!" and raised an arm as if to strike her.

"Not the face!" She heard a voice yell. "The pretty ones bring the best price!"

Her guard snarled and shoved her ahead of him towards the tunnel. It didn't matter where they were going. She had his knife.

Laila is not going to sit around all day and wait to get saved by Dash. She is taking care of business on her own, and now she has a knife. Let me put the little glinty lines on the sharp edge. This drawing looks great. As for Dash, he had better up his game if he is going to keep up with her.

Chapter 20

In the chaos and noise Dash walked through the crowd, following the flow. A couple of guards rushed past him towards the arena. He shouldered the gun, to fit in with the guards, who did not have any particular uniform. The weapon was the uniform.

The main tunnel was a long downhill spiral, but there were all kinds of side tunnels too. Best stay on the main - there was Laila. One guard. Her wrists tied. Nothing. The problem was the crowd. He needed a diversion. The tunnel on his right was empty. He pressed the AK against his hip and fired a burst into nothingness. The crowd looked around in panic, and began to run in every direction. He pressed his back against the tunnel wall. Laila and her guard were just a few steps away.

Laila knew the panic was her chance. She yanked her wrists hard to break the frayed rope, then spun with the knife and plunged it into the guard's neck. In her peripheral vision she saw a hand and the butt of a gun hit the side of the guard's head. It was Dash.

"Let's go!" Dash grabbed her wrist.

"What about the others? There are so many women here!"

"We can't. It's impossible."

"At least set them free!" Laila's chin jutted out and her eyes flared.

"Okay warrior Queen," Dash laughed grimly and and changed direction, stepping over the dead guard. "Walk normal and no one will notice us. You are my prisoner!"

Dash poked the AK into her back and Laila held her wrists together and walked in front of him.

"Can you find your way back?" Dash asked.

"Yes. We must hurry."

"No. Walk with the flow."

No one was guarding the young girls now. Something else was going on.

Dash smashed the wood around the locks with the butt of the AK. It was harder than it looked. Laila helped the girls climb out and cut the ropes on their wrists with her bloody knife.

There was a guard station to one side. It had a table and chairs with bottled water and an abandoned deck of cards. Behind that a couple of cots and duffel bags and a few dog-eared magazines. Not much excitement guarding people in cages, Dash thought as he rolled two thread-bare blankets with the bottled water in the middle. He tied the ends and threw it over his shoulder, like a bandolier.

"I play Basra with my grandmother," Dash looked at the spilled playing cards with nostalgia.

"Does she let you win?"

"Never," Dash laughed as he stuffed the cards in his pocket. "Let's go!"

Laila covered her face with a scarf but they were interrupted by a larger explosion, dust and gravel fell from the rocks above. The smell of burning tar was strong and made their eyes sting.

Whatever Dash had done had made a big mess.

"Walk towards the chaos," Dash said, and glanced at Laila's bare and bloody feet. The worn stone floor in the caves was smooth, but outside would be bad.

Dash tried to read the crowd. It was not all in one direction, like leaving a football match, but most people were walking away from the smoke. Dash wanted to get closer to the smell, the main cavern, because that is where the tunnels to the outside would be. And the fighters. Of course the fighters.

This part of the mountain was lit, from bulbs strung along the ceiling. Generators! Dash realized the electricity must come from generators outside. Powered by diesel... oh, if only he could knock those out...

Ahead he saw fighters, coming this way, not concerned with the crowds right in front of them. They were young and fierce. True believers.

Dash noticed a small dark tunnel on his left. On instinct he grabbed Laila's wrist and they ducked into it. It was narrow, and not lit, but there was faint light in the distance. Black rock all around.

"Go first, be careful." Dash knocked off the safety on the AK and reminded himself to shoot low. The tunnel was narrow, they would only be able to come after them single file.

They went fifty paces and nothing happened.

"Listen!" Laila grabbed his arm.

"What?"

"Ocean. I can smell it. This tunnel must be for ventilation."

They went another fifty paces and the ocean sound became louder. Now the tunnel narrowed and they were on their hands and knees. Behind them there was shouting. They felt fresh ocean breeze in their faces.

Laila got there first. She looked back at Dash and shook her head.

"Let me see."

Laila pressed her spine into the rock. Dash's body rubbed against her as he squeezed past. She closed her eyes. Four vertical stories below them the waves crashed against the rocks.

"I'm sorry. My bad idea."

Dash lay on the cool stone with his eyes closed. He felt her lips against his. He opened his eyes, full of questions.

"I didn't want to die today."

"We're not going to die today."

Dash focused on a rock where the middle had been eaten away by erosion into a hole. "If we could tear these old blankets into strips, we could tie them into a rope, and anchor it on this rock..."

"And then, after all that work and hope, die on the rocks below..."

"Maybe."

"Can we rest for just a little while? I love listening to the sounds of the waves."

"Laila, that's it! The tide will go out! We'll be able to see the rocks below us if we climb down."

"When?"

"I don't know. I've never seen an ocean in my life. But they always talk about the tide in books. We have to wait.

It took a long time to tear and knot the blankets. Was it long enough? Strong enough? It was impossible to estimate. Hours later they were done, and yes, the tide was receding, but it was slow.

Then they heard noise and chaos behind them. From inside the mountain. "I'd best go back and check," Dash looked worried.

"They can't get in here, can they?"

"We did. They can come one at a time."

"How many bullets do you have?"

"I don't know. Not enough. I can block up the tunnel with bodies. That will slow them down. Keep an eye on the tide."

Dash twisted his body and crawled into the darkness. Fifty yards and he realized he was not alone. Something was coming. He could tell by the sour smell of death that it was a scorpion, and the scraping. They must have brought a smaller one in a cage and released it into the tunnel. He held the AK steady and listened for the scraping sound, the clicking of the pincers. He lay flat. If his bullets hit the pincers they would be wasted. He had to get it dead center. He was at the narrowest point in the tunnel where the scorpion should not be able to arch its tail.

His plan was to fire a burst into the middle of the darkness. But then he realized the trick. His shooting would prove they were in this tunnel, they hadn't wanted to risk a man. Then they would fire into the tunnel.

His only chance was that they would have no way of knowing what the hungry scorpion would do if it felt that it couldn't strike. Dash had no idea, but he knew he couldn't shoot. He began crawling backwards towards Laila, draw the scorpion in, pray for the tide.

"They've sent a scorpion into the tunnel."

"And you couldn't shoot without giving up our position."

"Exactly."

"Drink some water."

Dash did that. "How does our tide look?"

"Wet, but we have to go."

They drank some more. Laila went first, she was a good climber. They had tied knots in the blankets at intervals to help hang on. If they got down, they could go through the shallows under cover of darkness towards the fishing dock.

Dash prayed the little boat he had seen was still there, and that the fighters would not realize where they had gone. It would take them a long time to search all the tunnels.

The old blankets were a blessing also, because they could at least dry their hands. The spray from the ocean meant the rocks were always wet and greasy. It got worse as they descended.

In the end, they made it, jumping the last two meters into soft wet sand. It was night. Little crabs scuttled under their feet. Dash picked up several and ate them.

"Gross."

"What? I'm hungry."

"Gross."

"I bet you eat sushi. What's the difference?"

"Your hands are bleeding," Laila touched his arm again.

"I didn't notice."

They stayed in the dark shadows at the base of the cliff for a moment, catching their breath, then crept through the rocks and sand where more small crabs scuttled. The foam from the waves was receding.

Dash did not want to go close to the dock, for fear of lights and guards. The fishing boats floated beyond the surf.

Dash's little boat was there, its outline a smooth arc. They caught their breath for a minute and Dash looked out at the surf line. They would have to walk it out that far, keeping their heads down. Dash unhooked the single rope that held the boat to a rock.

"Other side, stay low, don't make a silhouette."

Soon enough they were up to their waists, then shoulders. They weren't going to make it out past the surf line, even with the tide helping them.

"Can you swim?" Laila asked over the waves.

"No."

"Get in the boat and stay low. I can swim."

Laila held the boat steady while Dash climbed in with a thump. Laila tried to time the swell for some lift and with the last of her strength heaved herself into the boat, landing on the small of Dash's back.

"Ugh..."

"Shh..."

"Pardon?

They both lay in the bottom of the boat just long enough to realize it was full of water and their weight was not helping.

"Bail!"

"With what?"

"Then just stay low!" Dash pulled the rope starter on the ancient Johnson 6 horsepower motor. Nothing happened. Dash shook the gas can. It was almost full. Ok. Shift lever up. Ok. This is a very basic engine... primer bulb! Dash squeezed the bulb on the gas line a couple of times, then yanked the cord again. Nothing. Choke!

He pulled out the choke and then hit the starter hard.

Vroom! Ok. Maybe not vroom, it was 6 horsepower, intended simply for ferrying a couple of passengers or gear out to the small boats. Dash risked a look at the shoreline. Yes, he saw a couple of flashlights swinging and searching the rocks. Time to go. The sound of the surf would drown out the little engine.

Dash had never driven a boat, but he had no time to contemplate that as the surf was on them. It was pure luck that Dash hit the waves on an angle or they would have swamped. Then they were through, and Dash managed to get out past the fishing boats. He turned parallel to the shore and headed north. He practiced steering and adjusting the throttle. Speed was no good if they ran out of gas. They kept their heads low and settled into a slow and steady speed. The dark protected them.

He looked around and took stock of their resources. One assault rifle with unknown bullets left, and one automatic pistol, no extra clips, the clothes they were wearing - and of course no shoes. He had lost his sandals somewhere. The knife Laila had stolen, a four liter jug of water, half full, plus their own small bottles, a four meter coil of rope attached to a metal clip, and a plastic bucket. A cheap foam cooler with a towel and a t-shirt stuffed in it. Two small oars. One of the oar locks was broken, of course. They would have to paddle, one on each side, if it came to that.

"We'll take turns bailing and steering," he said, handing Laila the bucket.

Laila bailed. Dash leaned back to look at the stars and ensure they were headed north. Looking behind them, they could see only darkness.

Beyond the surf line the ocean was calm, the buzz of the engine was soothing.

Dash could not help but look at Laila's bare feet and legs, scratched, bruised, bloody, but still beautiful.

"In America they have an expression that cats have nine lives," Laila began. "You are turning me into a cat, every time you save me."

"You were doing quite well saving your own life, Laila, the way you took out that guard."

"I can't believe I put a knife into a person."

"Not a person. A demon... it's almost over," Dash spoke softly. At dawn we'll go back to land. We'll find a good spot and hide, then we can sleep."

"Are we safe?"

"I don't think they would ever imagine us getting away by boat," Dash tried to sound encouraging. "I trust they will be looking everywhere else."

"I overheard that they are digging some tunnel to free a demon."

"That's what I was doing all week, while you were locked in a box. We were lucky they didn't know who you were." Dash's eyes narrowed.

"Who am I?"

"Maybe your uncle can answer these questions."

"The bottom is pretty dry now. I can steer for a while, why don't you rest?"

Dash nodded. "Keep the land on your right and the ocean on your left and we're good."

Dash lay down in the bottom of the boat, making a pillow out of the towel and the soggy tee-shirt that smelled of gasoline and worse. He didn't care. It was like the best feather bed he'd ever met.

Chapter 21

They ran out of gas near dawn. How far they had come was unknowable, but the landscape had changed, the mountains had slid back into the earth, this was a coastal plain.

It was not too hard to row through the surf line to shore, the waves were going that way anyway. The risk was not getting sideways, but they learned.

Dash dragged the rowboat up on the beach and together they pulled it up under some palm trees in the shade. It was good to be warm as the sun dried their clothes. Dash slept again, one hand on his gun, one hand wrapped in Laila's fingers.

Hours later, they awoke and drank coconut water, Dash cracking them on a rock with the butt of his rifle. They tried to gnaw at the meat but it was difficult.

"You washed the knife, right?"

"Yes, here... I couldn't look at his face."

"He would not have hesitated to kill you, Laila."

"All those young girls..."

"Yes. It's very bad."

"I heard a car," Laila raised her head.

Dash frowned. "Maybe."

They climbed up the rocks behind the beach, the Atlas Mountains were miles in the distance. How long ago had that mountain adventure been?

There was a weary beach road, no signs to be seen.

"We can hitch-hike, but not with the rifle," Dash announced gravely as he pulled his shirt out of his pants to hide the handgun. I wish we had something to wrap it in."

"Show me how to shoot," Laila asked. "There is no one."

"Okay." Dash nodded and checked the clip.

"Tight on your shoulder. Kill a fish... I'm hungry."

Crack.

Crack.

Crack.

"Keep the barrel down."

Laila emptied the clip. "It hurts."

"You get used to it... now we'll just bury it in the sand. Hope kids don't find it."

Laila poured coconut water into the plastic jug. It would have to do.

After an hour they got a ride in the back of a farmer's truck. He would be passing through Laila's uncle's town in a few hours. Dash gave the man the last of his paper money, and thanked him and climbed in the back, laying down in the warm sun. What a sight they must have been.

"When we get to uncle's, I'm done, right?"

"When I was in that cage, scared out of my mind, I distracted myself by thinking about our last night. I knew you would come."

Dash blushed the color of sunset. "We're kids. Your family has big plans ."

"Are you not attracted to me?"

"It's got nothing to do with attraction. I promised your father."

"So that's why he wanted Addi to sleep in the middle — what did you promise him?"

"That I would take you to your uncle's.

"Don't you think about it? About us?"

"I've been concentrating on how to keep us from dying." Dash spoke gruffly and turned his back on her.

He did not want her to see how red his face was.

The sun was high when they got to the beautiful beach town. The streets were empty, silent, there were no shadows anywhere. They found the villa near the ocean, an easy walk to the beach.

Dash knew he should be happy. He had accomplished his mission. It was over, but still his heart sank in his chest.

Dash held Laila's hand tight and stared into her eyes. He was unable to speak.

A servant opened the door and stared at them in horror.

"Go and beg in the medina," she snorted.

"Uncle Taha, is he here?" Laila spoke with impressive dignity and in the most formal language. "It is I, Laila Ammon de la Finestere, speak this to Uncle Taha, please."

The woman stared, doubtful, hesitant. "Wait."

"Wait?" Dash laughed, he was light-headed from exhaustion, then realized he was still holding Laila's hand and let go.

A different servant, a man, came to the gate. He beckoned to Laila to enter, but put up his hand to bar Dash.

"May I plug in my phone?" Laila began. "Is Uncle here?"

"He must go to the Hammam," the servant said, gesturing to his right with his chin, by way of explanation to Laila, who shrugged and smiled at Dash.

"I have no money," Dash opened his hands in a gesture of penury.

The servant sighed and after quite a delay returned with a fifty dirham note and a bottle of mineral water. It would be sufficient for the bathing supplies and the bath house.

"I have no clean clothes. Please."

The servant stared at Dash's blood-stained, salt-encrusted, shredded garments with utter disgust and disappeared again. After a further delay the woman brought him a folded white djellaba, underthings, and a pair of sandals, then closed the gate in his face.

Chapter 22

The hamman was not far. The clerk stared at him but accepted his fee. In the changing room Dash's first problem was the gun. If it was discovered the police would certainly come.

He wrapped it discretely in his bloody old clothes (which no one would touch) and wrapped both inside of an extra towel he had rented, with his new things folded on top.

Dash spent an hour in the hot room, sweating, drinking mineral water and scrubbing his body with rhassoul, a lava clay he had bought at the front desk. His skin came off in layers: salt, blood, sand.

He had to use more water than was considered polite, but no one said anything. They were too busy sneaking glances at his chest, which had healed to the point of dark scabs exactly in the shape of the bear's paw. Ferrous's foot print. He was marked for life.

The other customers were too unnerved by his wounds to offer to scrub his back, a common courtesy which only required returning the favor. Still hurting from the burns from the hot tar, he didn't mind.

It was over. He had delivered Laila. He would ask her uncle for enough money to journey on to try and find his parents. He tried not to think about saying good-bye.

Dash found a mirror and then, using scissors he had borrowed at the front desk, he rough-cut his hair. Then he dressed and stood in front of the mirror. The white djellaba almost glowed against his coppery sun-burnt skin. Did he look like a typical young man again? A medical student perhaps, not a smuggler of women, a robber of the dead? Maybe, except for his sapphire eyes which burned with an intimidating frozen fire.

He returned the scissors, leaving the desk clerk his few remaining dirham as a gratuity and carried his old and bloody clothes in a paper bag under his arm. He wanted to toss them, but in the new loose garment he had nowhere to put the gun. He felt much better after washing, but faint and wobbly from not having eaten for several days. He couldn't remember their last meal. The handful of little crabs didn't count.

Dash could see the tiled turquoise walls of the villa, the yellow-flowered vines growing over them, the faded green Renault sedan parked beside it, the open gate - the air shimmering in the heat. It was so pretty. He could also see three men leading Laila out of the gate. Her hands were tied behind her back and she had a rope around her neck.

Chapter 23

You didn't really think that just because Dash defeated a giant scorpion, rescued Laila and blew up half the joint his troubles were going to be over? You don't win a girl like Laila that easily. We are just getting warmed up my friends. I looked up at Mr. Mulch. He was still reading his thick book. Laila was reading hers and had kicked off her shoes.

The fake Swede was passing Laila love notes right here in detention! I'm assuming they are love notes, and he is not asking her questions about physics or Moroccan hair products. This is not good. But it's okay, I can protect Laila from this jerk. I'm the one with the sharp pencil.

Chapter 24

Dash didn't think Laila saw him. The first man held the back door open, the second shoved her inside. The third kept watch. His eyes locked with Dash's as Dash dropped to one knee, steadying his weapon. The sun beat a hard flat light, he squinted. There were three men, or was it six?

Crack.

The watchman dropped like a stone. The green Renault sputtered to life and drove away, leaving their wounded colleague writhing on the ground. Dash had no shot without risking hitting Laila. Why had he left her alone? Why?

He ran to the wounded man who had both hands grasping his thigh. Dash stood over him, kicking his gun into the street.

"How did you find her?"

"We have been watching the house," he gasped.

"Where are they taking her?"

"Are you the one... the one who killed a giant scorpion in single combat?" The man asked, an astonished look on his face.

"I was lucky," Dash said, "luckier than you." He frowned, wondering how the man knew this story. When had it been? Yesterday? Two days before? "Where will they take her?"

"You weren't lucky," the man snorted. "You are cursed. Now you have unleashed hell."

"Cursed? Do you hear me arguing with you? Where are they taking her," Dash pressed on the man's wound with his foot.

"The village bleu, of course. In the north. There is a café, Café Americain - try the falafel..."

"You're hilarious. Who took her?"

"Who do you think?" the man coughed. "The bride? The Kahina? You can't imagine what she is worth."

Dash frowned. What? Laila was no one's bride. "Are you ready for paradise?" Dash asked without irony as he pressed the gun against the man's head. "Make peace with God."

The man did not answer. His eyes were closed. Dash stopped. He put the safety back on and went through the man's pockets. Several thousand dirham, mostly small bills, perhaps the first half of his fee for the kidnapping. And a cheap cell phone, which he also took along with the clip from the man's weapon.

It was plain enough what had happened once Dash had dragged the man inside and leaned him against a wall in the shade.

The uncle and the servants had been lined up in the courtyard and shot. The house had been ransacked for valuables to make it look like a robbery. No one would know a kidnapping had occurred, because no one living knew Laila was there – except Dash and the people who had taken her.

The local police would decide it was a robbery and two could share the take more easily than three. He doubted this man would talk to the police, and the file would be closed.

"What is your name?"

"Ahmed Marwa," he said, grimacing with pain.

"I'm not going to kill you," Dash announced, "but the police will come. And this doesn't look... good," gesturing at the bodies. "Did you and your friends do this?"

Marwa did not answer, so Dash left him in the courtyard and went back inside. He grabbed a piece of warm bread and two bottles of cold tea in the kitchen. Lunch had been in preparation. The table was already set - for two.

He found the dead uncle's bedroom. They were about the same size. He needed to change. Western clothes. Dash put on sneakers, they fit. Then a dark linen suit over a plain white t-shirt. He found a belt, pulled it extra tight and stuck his gun in the small of his back. He found a money clip in the night table the kidnappers had missed. Maybe five thousand dirham. The thugs had taken any jewelry, but it was ok. He had enough.

In the closet he found a small Addidas duffel bag. He packed underwear and extra t-shirts. Some disinfectant and bandages from the bathroom.

He could hear sirens warbling in the distance. The local police would be no balls of fire, but they would be nasty enough in person. It was time to go. He left Ahmed Marwa a bottle of cold tea, and returned the money he had taken, which was received with colorful curses.

Dash walked in a relaxed way, eating his bread, heading towards the center of town. He found a café in the medina with plenty of tourists for cover and ordered food. The police would be watching the bus and train stations. This murder would be a big story, the uncle had been a wealthy man. It was strange that he had chosen to not spend any money on bodyguards. Or perhaps those men had been the bodyguards, and betrayed their master. He had no way of knowing.

Dash ate, dipping roast chicken in fiery harissa and savoring each bite. He could not think without food, but he did not want to over-eat and get cramps. He had time to think his bitter thoughts. Here he was. He had lost Laila, and again was reduced to robbing the dead to survive. Maybe they didn't care.

Dash chatted with a young American couple at the next table, thinking it was hilarious that just a few days ago he spoke little English, but since Cleo had bitten him he just heard the words in his head and understood. The couple drove him to the next town where he checked into a student hostel for the night, electing to sleep on the roof, where it would be cooler. He had become used to sleeping outside. He needed to think. He had about 5,000 dirham and 6 bullets plus one clip of 9 more.

If he was careful, he had enough money to get to Tangier. What obligation did he have to Laila? He had delivered her. How was he supposed to go up to Chefchaouen and find Laila in some café?

"Go to the blue café," the kidnapper had said. "Try the falafel."

"That's no help. Everything is blue there."

The kidnappers would not harm Laila, he decided. They would call her father and he would ransom her. That was how such things worked. It was not

Dash's problem, he had no money to pay ransom anyway. And anyway he didn't have her father's number.

The problem was his heart ached and he missed her. He didn't want her to be frightened. He could take the train. These and many other unsound thoughts wandered through Dash's brain like lost children. He prayed that Baz had arrived at their village. Finally he slept.

Chapter 25

The train took all day, and despite napping Dash was still exhausted. He decided it was worth the fee to have the petit-taxi driver find the Café Americain which, after many winding streets and a five minute walk in the medina, he was successful. His feet, cut up from the escape, made walking painful. Inside, Dash ordered tea and sat inside. It cost more to sit outside.

Dash watched the waiter as he loaded each tray and took it to the tables. Most of the customers were tourists sitting on the terrace. The waiter took a tray and went to stairs in the back corner and started up. Dash was behind him in no time, pressing his gun into the man's back.

"How many?"

"Three," the man sneered. "You have no chance."

Dash lifted the cloth to see how many plates were there. Two.

"If you warn them, you die first."

The man proceeded up the stairs and rapped his knuckles sharply on the door. There was no way of knowing if it was a warning signal.

"Salut," a voice called out.

"Bravo, mon amis," said a man in a gravelled, calm voice, slowly clapping his hands and nodding. He was alone in the room. He was older, European looking, with a sharp nose and longish gray hair brushed back, a trimmed gray-beard wearing a blue and white striped pullover, as a French sailor might. His face had an impressive assortment of scars, and his brown eyes danced. He looked more like an eccentric musician than a gangster.

"You found me," he put his hands up in a mock gesture of surrender. "Serve the last supper," he said to the waiter with a grin.

Dash just stared while the waiter set out the food and left.

"Shall we eat and talk like civilized men? My digestion will be better if you put your gun on the floor."

Dash did that and sat. "How did you know I would come?" Dash tried to sound cool.

"How did I know you would want a Niçoise...?" The man snorted and raised his eyebrows, smiling. "I would have come for Laila - and I'm an old man. Anyway, our Niçoise is famous."

"How did you know I was coming?"

"I was informed when you entered the café."

"And you were confident that I would eat with you instead of killing you?"

"I am Gattopardo. Bon appetite." He began eating. "And you are?"

"Dash Lahlou."

"And you are the one who brought Miss Laila Ammon de la Finestere from the end of the world?"

"Yes."

"Impressive. But you know that. Why?"

"I was asked. By her father and the elders of my village."

"You were not paid?"

"No."

"You truly came through the mountains?"

"Yes."

"It was difficult?"

That was a question too dumb to dignify with an answer, but Dash realized that it was not asked stupidly, but to see how Dash answered. After a moment Dash felt he had to say something.

"The Niçoise is excellent," he began. "As for the mountains, I have done it before, with my uncles when I was young. But not the highest route, we had to do that because of the rebels."

"Would you like to be paid for such work? Taking people or valuable things through the mountains?"

"I have never thought about it. I would not carry drugs."

"Have I asked you to carry drugs?"

"No," Dash admitted.

"I followed your journey through rebel reports as they hunted you. Do you know what havoc you created in the their encampment?

"Good."

"Yes. By the way, how did you escape? They have not yet figured that out."

"We were lucky. First, their mountain is an ancient volcano, there are all kinds of small tunnels, too small to be useful except for ventilation. We could smell the sea, so that's how we got out. I had seen a small boat that supplied the fishing boats. No one would think of it."

"Luck seems to be something you have in abundance – wine?" Gattopardo offered to pour from a carafe of rosé.

"No, thank you - are you not with the rebels?" Dash was puzzled.

"They were a sometimes client, years ago. Black market weapons." Gattopardo shrugged. "Now they are too crazy, in too much of a hurry to meet God."

"Who is in a hurry to meet God?"

"Oh, those fellows... I myself have the patience of stones, on that topic. It is not a conversation I look forward to."

"What are they doing there, anyway, do you know?"

"They are digging inside the volcano. Their plan is to meet Lucifer half-way."

"You are not serious!"

"They believe there is a demon," Dash explained, "what they call a *Jinn*, wrapped in chains, trapped in a cave who would be grateful to be released. From my observation, there are hundreds of caves inside the volcano, but they don't know where to dig. The true believers supervise the slaves. The true believers are the fighters who raid the villages for slaves and supplies and for women and children to sell in the slave market. The lucky ones get to be brides for the fighters."

"Oh, I believe in Jinn, if that is who they are looking for. It can't be pleasant being trapped between being a man and a god. But who knows?" Gattopardo shrugged. "I have not met too many devils - wives excepted, of course."

Dash had to laugh. He did not know what to take seriously. "Did you kill Laila's uncle?"

Gattopardo sighed, and spread his hands in mild exasperation. "It is customary, my friend, it is politesse... to save such questions for after the meal, until we are enjoying the sweet, the espresso, perhaps a digestif... but you are young and in a hurry... I understand. I was in a hurry once too. So, though it grieves me to deprive you of the entire elegant saga..." Gattopardo made an exaggerated gesture with his hands. "Uncle Taha paid me a fine sum to kidnap Laila. Why would I kill him? Laila says he was dead when she got there, when you were sent to the hamman to bathe."

Chapter 26

Gattopardo sat back, enjoying the shock on Dash's face.

"Dead Uncle Taha... paid you... to kidnap his own niece?"

"Yes."

"Why?" Dash asked incredulously. "That makes no sense. We were going there anyway!"

"For ransom, of course."

"He is her uncle!"

"Every family has a black sheep," Gattopardo grinned. "Even mine!"

Gattopardo poured himself a second glass of wine. "Laila's uncle, Taha, was heavily in debt to some unsavory characters, worse than me! I know that's hard to believe... and though he had negotiated Laila's marriage to the Prince, he would not profit from it in the short term... I imagine they had run out of patience with not getting paid, so they decided to kill him."

"Marriage to the Prince?" Dash stared at Gattopardo.

"The marriage of Laila Ammon de la Finistere to, Abbas, the Prince Facile, first in line to the throne of Morocco... do you not follow social media?" Gattopardo stared at Dash with an innocently raised eyebrow.

"I've been... busy..." Dash's heart crashed in this chest.

"Shall I continue?"

"Perhaps I will take a glass of wine, thank you." Dash had never had a glass of wine in his life, but he'd seen men take a drink in films, when they had bad news.

"It is light but fruity, enough acid to be refreshing - from my own vineyard," Gattopardo said, beside himself with amusement at the look on Dash's face. We sell a lot of it in the café."

Dash took a sip, it was good. "Tell me about the Prince."

"The Prince receives a modest allowance. He has no real political or financial muscle. Enter the southern rebels. Their leader is obsessed with the legend of Laila being the direct descendant of the female warrior Queen and sorceress, Kahina - and for Laila's purity - that she is, in short - a virgin."

Gattopardo eye-balled Dash, whose face turned as pink as the rosé, then to red and back to pink.

"I see," nodded Gattopardo. "L'amour propre – how old are you?"

"Sixteen. Laila is sixteen. We are kids."

"Well, I am sorry to tell you this, but Taha's plan was for me to kidnap her, gently, then claim the rebels had taken her. The King would pay the ransom, Taha would stage manage the whole thing, and Taha's share would be enough to solve his financial problems—aren't families delightful?"

"Is this what people do in the cities?"

"Uncle got greedy."

Dash stared at him.

"I was against it, of course," Gattopardo said. "The rebels are too crazy now to deal with, even for me. I don't want anything to do with them, but both the rebels and the King understand the publicity value with the people of North Africa in having Laila as their hero, or at least for now, 'Queen-in-waiting'. For the rebels it would help legitimize them politically. Fulfilling the ancient prophecy of uniting North Africa under one beloved ruler."

"You are making my head spin. Laila is safe?"

"Yes, yes," Gattopardo waived his hand. "But I can't protect her if the rebels find out I have her. I'm not set up for it. I don't want their money."

"And this involves me how?"

"Here is my offer - you can have Laila back under two conditions: you must take her to the Prince, and you must convince her to leave me out of whatever story you weave."

"Why can't you just take her to the Prince?"

"I would be blamed and arrested. You kids must speak nothing to the Prince about Uncle Taha and what happened, just say you got there too late and saw the bodies. As for you, consider coming to work for me. You have natural talent. The rest I can teach you."

"I have no desire to hurt anyone."

"I am talking smuggling. I am mainly in the kief, or hashish trade. It is easy and profitable. Then I invest in real estate and colorful tourist cafés, where I sell my own fruity rosé. I am vertically integrated, as they teach in American business schools. I don't touch cocaine, that is another drug that makes people crazy. As for killing people? It is rare, and anyway I don't need you for that."

"I don't want to do any of those things," Dash sipped his wine. "I am a student. At least I want to be. I was preparing to write my exams when all this happened."

"What can you do, Dash? Go back to your village and wait? Your village may not exist anymore. I have no facts either way, but I have no confidence that the rebels will respect the long tradition of neutrality for which The Oasis is rightfully renowned."

Dash's heart sank. He had feared as much.

"My parents were in Tangier when I left. I guess a month ago. Maybe six weeks."

"Do you know where they are? Have you heard from them?"

"No," Dash admitted.

"I have contacts there, it is not so far. If I can locate your parents, or at least a lead, would you consider that a gesture of good will on my part?"

"Yes, of course."

"So be it."

"Do you need pocket money?"

"No," Dash sipped his wine. But I am running out of bullets."

Gattopardo slapped the table as he laughed. "The man who does not want to kill is nearly out of bullets. May I write that down? It is a wonderful expression."

He got up and went to a desk drawer and extracted two 9 mm clips.

"Thank you," Dash smiled. "Laila, when can I see her?"

"Not tonight, but probably tomorrow late. Let me do my work. There is preparation. Laila is a delight, in case you did not know."

Dash leaned down to pick up his own weapon from the ground and checked that the clips fit. "What about your man, Ahmed Marwa. I didn't kill him. I imagine the police have him."

"I will take care of that," Gattopardo said. "His family are on salary, whether he is in jail, or with me, so he will not give any useful information to the police. I take care of my people," he said.

"I am not your enemy," Dash sighed. "I want Laila to be safe, I want to find my parents, and I want to go to school. Is that so much?"

"It's not so much the object of desire that becomes the burden, but the desire itself," Gattopardo's expression went from contemplative to laughing in a split second. "It must be the wine, I sound like a philosopher!"

Dash laughed too. Against all his better judgment he liked Gattopardo. He could have sat there all day listening to his stories.

"There is a riad at the corner, my young friend. The door is behind the orange trees. They are holding a room for you. You are my guest. You can walk around, but stay in our little neighborhood and rest, I may need you on short notice. Contemplate our conversation. I will be in touch."

Dash nodded and stood up.

Gattopardo stood also and offered his embrace which Dash accepted. "Fate has turned over a card for us. Let's play our hands well."

He walked Dash to the door. "And by the way, so that your suspicion is eased, the man and woman at Uncle's house? They were not real servants. I do not generally go around shooting the help - unless they screw up, of course!" Gattopardo laughed. "They were guards who belonged to Uncle Finestere's creditors, to make sure he didn't try and leave the country. He was a prisoner in his own house."

"I appreciate the explanation."

"Did you truly not know... that Laila is promised to marry the Prince?" Gattopardo asked, his voice quiet.

Dash's eyes got large. "A month in the mountains together, peril at every turn, captured by rebels, a long night in an open boat..." Dash shrugged. "Strangely, the topic never came up."

"What did she tell you?"

"She is to be an angel of mercy. Distributing relief supplies to villages."

"Don't hurry to judge her, my friend... she may not even know the plans her family made." Gattopardo poured more rosé. "In our culture, which is torn between millennia, this is not unusual. And anyway—Gattopardo's mouth twisted—how many of us know our true fate in advance? It is said that even Lucifer was once an angel."

'Lucifer was once an angel.' Gattopardo is hilarious. I am drawing him right now. I should write that down, too. Okay, obviously I am obviously cutting Dash a huge break here, letting him make a friend in Gattopardo, but it's not realistic that Dash can do everything, not that he doesn't try. And we have to keep Laila safe. I have to keep her in peril of course to impress her when she reads this, but in peril she is, now that Sven the fake Swede has shown his hand. Finestere the Minister of the Interior, her father, is going to want a big say in what Laila does. And how does Dash know he can trust Gattopardo? After all, he just kidnapped Laila like five minutes ago. Can Dash be convinced by a sandwich? I mean I could, I admit it, but Dash? Okay, it wasn't a sandwich, it was a Niçoise. I'm not even sure what that is but I bet it is something Laila would eat all the time so I'm mentioning it. Maybe I'll look up what it is and I can drop it in casual conversation. "Oh, I had a Niçoise for lunch, what did you have?"

Chapter 27

Dash found the riad on a street with busy cafés and shops and many tourists. He was treated with deference and given a small attractive room looking out over the courtyard. To him, it was a palace. A ceiling fan spun. Dash sipped mineral water and enjoyed a plate of mandarins, almonds and honeyed walnuts, but his brain did not relax as he tried to figure out what he had learned.

Either Gattopardo really was trying to recruit him, or he was just stalling while Laila was in transit, being delivered to the final buyer. Where was Cleo the Asp to advise him? All this turmoil in his brain kept him from enjoying the hospitality. In the end he pulled the blankets off the bed and lay on the floor. Having slept hard for so many nights, it was the only way he was comfortable.

Dash woke with the light, then went down to breakfast in the courtyard. No sign of Laila or Gattopardo. He spent the day in his room, sleeping, then walked around the neighborhood in the evening. He needed time to think.

He ate in a café from which he could watch people come and go from Gattopardo's Café. His appetite for food shocked even him. Finally he went back to the riad. At last there was a message. "Come down for breakfast at eight - G". Finally he slept.

The next morning Laila was at a good table, peeling mandarin slices with her beautiful fingers. She was wearing new clothes, a rainbow which faded against her eyes. The table was set for three, with pastries, breads, yogurt and fresh honey, and fruits.

"Are you safe?" Dash stood over her, relief rushing through his body.

"Yes, our new friend has kept his word."

Dash sat and Laila poured tea for him. "He took me shopping. That's why I didn't see you yesterday."

"Shopping?"

"Bath, hair, nails, clothes, a nice lunch, though it didn't start so well. I was blind-folded, a terrible car ride," Laila leaned forward dramatically. "I woke up in a stone cellar tied to a chair. Gattopardo walks in and unties me, takes off my blindfold, then says "Let's go shopping.""

"What did you say?"

"Can we have lunch first?"

"He's a character. Do you believe him?" Dash whispered.

"About Uncle? I am spitting with anger if it is true. My father always excused uncle's eccentricities. I expected Gattopardo to lie, but he just told me the story in a plain way... and... I think it is too horrible to not be true. Were this a simple kidnapping I would have been kept in the trunk of a car and it would have been over by now, don't you think? I would be dead or delivered."

"I don't know what to think. I believe him, but I wish Cleo would advise us."

"Does she talk to you still?"

"Not lately, when she does I just get ideas in my head. It is disconcerting."

"I miss you. At night I miss you more," Laila discreetly brushed her hand over his. Laila blushed, "where did you sleep?"

"I slept here the last two nights..." Dash hesitated. "Laila, I had no shot, when they took you..."

"I know. I was so scared they would shoot at you," Laila looked away. "Gatto has been nothing but polite, and has apologized many times for our original meeting... I... saw the execution of the servants."

"Did you see me? The idiot in white, running?"

"You killed one of them, didn't you?"

"Wounded. If I had come five minutes sooner..."

"It might have been worse..." Laila shook her head. "Don't blame yourself. You honored my father, Dash, you did everything he asked.

Almost everything, Dash thought bitterly. "Did Gattopardo tell you that your uncle was a prisoner? That the servants were guards, sent by people to whom he owed money?"

"No, but that explains why they were so rude."

"I wish we knew the truth."

"Yes. The truth. Dash, if you want to go on, I understand. You have no obligation to me. I know you are worried about your parents."

Dash stared into the deep well of her eyes.

"Did you know... Laila... about the Prince?"

"I suspected. I tried not to think about it. But I didn't care until I met you."

Dash had to look away. He squeezed an almond between his fingers until it broke.

"Gattopardo is arranging the palace," Laila continued. "I guess it is delicate."

"Does your father know what has happened?"

"I am sure by now he knows that uncle is dead, the rest..." Laila left her thoughts hanging in the air. "I will talk to him soon, I discussed it with Gattopardo."

"If I were the Prince, I would declare a city-wide day of feasting and cover the street to the palace with flower petals," Dash gestured with animation.

Laila blushed red and covered her face with her long fingers and then dropped her gaze.

"Will you take me to the Prince? I know you don't have to... will you do it, not for my father ~- will you do it for me?"

Dash knew he could walk away now with a clear conscience, but... yes he would deliver Laila to the palace, and say goodbye. He could do it.

"Yes."

Laila leaned forward and whispered, her eyes were the clearest of emeralds. "What's going to happen to us?"

"Thirty minutes, kids, eat up, it's a long drive," Gattopardo stood over them, this morning in a navy business suit with a dark knit tie.

"Good morning," Laila said, while Dash nodded, not liking the interruption.

Gattopardo sat down and leaned forward. "In an hour a dark, four door Peugeot will be out front. Bring out your things. The driver is a discrete and reliable man who is not known to be an associate of mine. He will drive you to Rabat, but not to the main palace. He has an envelope he will open when you enter Rabat as to the final destination.

The Prince Facile is at Dra es Salaam, a smaller palace which is more private. At a particular café you will meet a senior member of the Royal Guard who will discretely take you into the palace. At that point Miss Laila will be the responsibility of the Royal Guard, and you and I, Dash, will be free."

Dash's face was all business, but his stomach churned. Gattopardo put a cell phone in Dash's breast pocket and clapped him on the shoulder to give him courage. "Call me when it's over, don't forget."

Laila watched Dash as Gattopardo spoke. Did Dash know that the night they had spent in the boat, while Dash slept, she had spent most of her time staring at him, her heart breaking?

Chapter 28

Dash and Laila both sat in the back. It was the furthest Dash had ever driven in a private car. The driver was a large older man in a black suit who did not speak beyond providing them with water.

They were nervous to talk, even in English, not knowing what the driver might understand. The radio murmured, though the news was anything but, for three different cafés had already been bombed that day, one in Fez and two in Tangier. Credit was claimed by the rebels, who had issued a pronouncement that the cities were a "plague zone" infested by western influence. The announcer continued that the government was allocating additional military resources to hunting them.

Dash stared out the window. Laila fell asleep on his shoulder, her fingers entwined with his. He wondered if the driver could see them in his mirror, he decided he didn't care.

He didn't want to sleep. He had a sense of foreboding that he might never see Laila again after today. He could not tell her that. No matter what happened, he would promise her anything.

Chapter 29

It was mid-afternoon when they arrived in Rabat, the capital. The driver seemed used to the crazy traffic and they wove their way to the popular Café La Comédie.

Dash thought it was smart to meet in such a public place, bustling with couples, tourists, business people taking a break. He could hear Arabic, French, Dutch, English. He could understand everything. The latest bombings had not deterred the customers. Laila stared at him, her eyes large.

The driver turned around for the first time and extended his open hand towards the back seat. Dash thought he wanted a tip.

"Gun."

"Ah..." Dash reluctantly extracted his weapon and handed it to the driver.

"Clips."

Dash did that also.

"Captain Asim, back corner. Red beret."

"Thank you," Dash inclined his head, though it had not been an epic conversation.

The man opened the back door for them and they got out, grateful to stretch their legs.

Inside, Captain Asim stood to greet them. Even in civilian clothes he looked like a soldier. Of course he wore the red beret of the Royal Guards. He was about thirty and sported a thin moustache and a thin scar on his cheek that would have looked good in an old movie. He stood up and held a chair for Laila, who looked around the café with delight noticing that many of the women were wearing modern western clothing. Tea appeared and several small plates of beautiful sweets. After their ordeal, the bounty was almost unimaginable.

Captain Asim removed his beret and folded it into a pocket of a jacket that hung on the back of his chair.

"I don't need to be conspicuous anymore," he looked at Dash with amusement, certain, from seeing him in person, that the stories of what this pretty boy had accomplished were exaggerated. How hard was it, after all, to walk through mountains when you had been doing it your whole life? As for the other stories, fighting rebels, battling giant scorpions, well, the truth of those remained to be seen.

Nonetheless he was relieved they had made it. The Prince Facile had been beside himself waiting for Laila, whom he had not seen in person since she was twelve years old.

After some friendly conversation about the long history of the famous café, Captain Asim began to explain what would happen now.

"Now we will go to Dra es Salaam - the little palace, we call it, where you will be able to refresh yourselves and where you will sleep tonight. There will be a small welcoming dinner, after which Laila will be taken to meet the Prince's parents - the King. Dash, you are invited to relax with the officers, cards... billiards... as is our custom, or you may retire to your room – of course you have been through a lot. Tomorrow, Laila has a very full day, and Dash, if you agree, our security analysts would like to hear about your encounters with the rebels, especially their encampment on the coast.

"I'm not sure where it was, aside from being a small fishing harbor on the ocean - and a mountain. It was just a bunch of huge caves and a sort of natural amphitheater they used."

"Don't worry, they will show you some maps and photos. We'll deal with that tomorrow. More tea?"

"Sure," both Dash and Laila nodded.

"Captain," Dash began, "I'm not getting my gun back, am I?"

"Civilians don't have weapons here. "Of course as your adventure was in the service of our country, no one is going to say anything. Do you have any papers?"

"I have nothing."

"You're an Algerian national, though, right?"

"Yes. Though I am a Berber. Countries come and go."

"So it seems. We'll take care of that, too. It will take a few days."

"Thank you. Excuse me," Dash stood up.

"Upstairs," Captain Amin said. "On the left."

Dash made his way up a wide spiral staircase. His heart was pounding as the end with Lala neared. He noticed that the second floor was a lounge, but it was not busy at all, on a couple of young male tourists playing dominoes. The thing that Dash noticed was that one of the fellow's hair was long and dirty blonde and tied in knots, he looked like a Swedish back-packer. No big deal, there were still plenty of hippies in Morocco.

Dash washed his face and stared into the mirror. His face was pale. Just exhaustion. If he could sleep for a week everything would be just fine. Anyway, it would be fun to see a real palace.

Then Dash heard yelling and a short burst of automatic weapons fire, then several single shots, and another burst. More yelling and screams. He opened the bathroom door. The tourist table was empty. The Swedish looking backpacker stood at the top of the stairs, an AK pointing down in case anyone tried to escape, and he had a good vantage point of the entire café, including the front door. But if he turned around he would see Dash.

The screams and yelling were louder. The Swede also had a hand gun stuck in the back of his pants. Dash didn't think. He leapt forward and grabbed for it with his right hand and shoved the man hard between the shoulder blades with his left. The man spun as he fell down the stairs and Dash could see his contorted, hateful face. Dash took off the safety and went down the stairs two at a time, pausing to look into the Swede's eyes, glazed with death.

Dash crouched to survey the café, everyone was staring the other way at the man with the female hostage. Most of the customers were frozen in place. Two security guards lay on the floor. There were two men standing. One had the hostage, the other surveyed the room, holding his weapon at waist height, sweeping it back and forth.

"Laila Ammon de la Finistere!" We know she is here!" He repeated it in Arabic and French. "We will kill a hostage every minute until she surrenders!"

Dash could see Laila and Captain Asim in the corner, her back was to the rebels. Dash could see Laila put her hands on the table, preparing to stand.

The hostage girl was crying and squirming, the rebel was yelling and waving his gun.

"All the females. Stand. All the men. Sit."

"It is not necessary. I am she," Laila announced loudly as she stood, pushed her chair back, and turned to face the man, her hands calmly at her sides.

The man cracked the hostage on her head and shoved her to the floor, then he gestured for Laila to walk towards him. Dash couldn't see Asim, as Laila was in the way, but he knew that Asim had no shot. He also remembered his promise to Laila's father, that he would not let her be taken alive.

I'm beginning to think the clock on the wall is broken, or maybe just discouraged. It has given up the ghost and this day will never end. As for us? We are where we began, Dash's impulsive promise to appease a crazy man, Laila's father, that if Laila were to be captured by the rebels it would be better if Dash killed her. Better?!

You know what? Dash has free will, and he doesn't want to kill anyone, though he did just kill the fake Swede Sven, though I don't consider that much of a loss. Saving Laila is going to have consequences. So right now Dash has to make the biggest choice of his young life. I need to sharpen my pencil for this one.

Chapter 30

Dash could feel his heart pounding as he sighted the gun. He would be spotted any second.

"Snake eyes baby, snake eyes."

Crack.

Crack.

Dash's bullet ripped through Laila's ear lobe and scraped her neck, then hit the rebel in the eye, which instantly became a black hole. He fell sideways onto a café table which collapsed. Dash's second bullet missed the other guy, but Captain Asim's didn't. A staccato burst of gunfire went into the ceiling as he fell. People screamed and cowered. Already there were sirens in the distance.

Laila turned and stared into Dash's eyes from across the room, her hand pressed against her bloody ear. Captain Asim jumped up and stood over the bodies, making sure they were dead, then talking urgently into his phone.

Dash shoved his gun into his waistband, then jumped over the railing. He grabbed a cloth napkin and pressed it against Laila's ear.

"You shot me!"

"Sorry. Keep this pressed against your ear."

"You shot me!"

"I'm sorry." Dash put his arms around her.

"I want to see the girl who was hurt."

Many customers were gathered around the hostage girl and the dead security guards. Pop music kept playing on the sound system.

Police were there in less than two minutes and Captain Asim conferred with them, pulling out his identification. Dash was pretty certain that a Royal Guards Captain had authority over the local police.

Laila crouched over the hostage, who was hysterical and touching the blood with her fingers. They helped her up and she sat with her friends, waiting for the medics.

Dash and Laila sat back down at their table, all the energy had drained out of their bodies, he could feel it. It was all just too much. Dash gave Laila a new napkin for her ear.

"I'm fine. You owe me new earings. Cute ones."

Wow, she's pissed, Dash thought.

Captain Asim came back and sat with them. Asim looked at Dash with new respect.

"Security Service is coming. Dash, how did you know?" He asked.

"They were just guys, playing dominoes upstairs, like at every café. I was just lucky to get behind the blonde. I called him the Swedish back-packer in my head... I never dreamed they were... I was just lucky."

"You killed two of them."

"Yeah, me who's not allowed to have a gun," Dash laughed and put the weapon in the middle of the table. He felt sick. Maybe the police would be able to figure out where the Swede had got it.

"You saved us. I had my gun in my lap, but Laila was between me and them. I couldn't have got both of them without the AK guy getting off a burst." Captain Asim stared at the floor. "People would have died before I could shoot."

"It was luck, Captain. I had to pee at just the right time – but the important thing – who knew we were meeting here? Who picked the spot? I'm not throwing stones, but either it was the driver who brought us - and he didn't open his envelope with the final destination until we were in the city, and I never saw him make a call - or someone talked on your end."

"We were betrayed, Captain." Laila spoke with authority. "I saw the look in his eyes. He had confidence, he knew I was here."

"Yes, it's bad. For now... let's get Laila to the hospital. At some point we will each have to give a statement."

Captain Asim introduced Dash to the local officer who would be in charge. The officer of course asked for Dash's papers, but Asim shook his head. "No papers."

The dead men lay on the floor with white table cloths over them.

Dash craned his neck around the room. "Crap, I think they killed our waiter."

Hundreds of people were milling around outside, but the police had established a perimeter with yellow tape. The crowd was anxious, today had been a bad day all over.

Dash, Laila and Captain Asim stood out of the way on the sidewalk. A black Peugot sedan appeared at the curb out of nowhere. Dash held the door for Laila and they were gone in a whoosh. Captain Asim was deep in conversation on his phone. Laila put her hand over Dash's.

"You were supposed to shoot me, weren't you?"

"That's ridiculous."

"I know my father. And I know when you are lying."

"Then I screwed up," he stared into her eyes, drowning.

"I thought we would both die," she said. "And I was okay with that."

Dash bit his lip. "I never killed anyone before," Dash whispered. "I never wanted to."

"They kill themselves, Dash. It's a death cult."

Dash gestured for the driver to pull over to the curb. He opened the car door and threw up. All those lovely pastries.

Okay. We are going into uncharted waters here. Dash saved Laila this time, but unleashed Hell. Even I am scared that this is going to get ugly. I looked up. Laila had put her book down and was resting her head on her arms. I had better keep an eye on her.

Chapter 31

It was a room where the servant was invisible, yet tea was offered and accepted and classical music played in the background. Dash sat on the edge of a long antique couch and waited as Laila's father, Monsieur Ammon de la Finestere, Minister of the Interior for Algeria, paced, aided by a carved walking stick. His beard had added some gray. Dash of course had not seen him, not since he and Laila had left The Oasis to cross the Atlas Mountains to Morocco on foot a month or so before. Is a month a long time? Maybe yes.

If the Minister recognized the navy linen suit that Dash wore as having belonged to his recently deceased brother Taha, he gave no sign. Perhaps he had bigger fish to fry. To Dash, Laila's father looked like a banker who didn't like the terms of a loan he'd made.

"How is your leg, Sir?"

"It aches at night, but they tell me the operation was a success."

"I'm glad."

The Minister lit a cigarette. "You did not keep your promise, Dash. The promise you made when I entrusted Laila to your care. Her experience was harrowing."

"You were in shock Sir, from the plane crash, and your injury. I did my best to protect Laila, and I'm sorry about her ear."

"You won't hear the end of that," Finestere grunted, as close to a laugh as he was likely to get.

"No..."

"It's not easy to bear such an obligation as I have towards you, Dash. The doctor has examined her, and she is fine. A few stitches for now, a bruise on her neck that her hair covers. She is either lucky or you are skilled. Or both... she can have plastic surgery later if necessary. Most of all, her honor is intact."

How do you not blush? Dash wondered, but luckily the Minister was preoccupied, maybe thinking how to get out of this awkward meeting.

"There will be a small dinner tonight, Dash. The Prince wants to thank you himself – and here," he reached for an envelope on the desk behind him. "Your new passport. I understand nothing personal survived your journey?"

"Only Laila's honor, Sir."

The Minister knew a better chess move when he heard it, so he changed the subject. "What are your plans now that your obligation to me is satisfied?"

"I need to write my final exam."

"Where are you thinking?"

"University 1, where my father taught. Or perhaps here in Rabat, Mohammed V, if that were possible, and eventually, medical school. Laila and I talked about that."

"Yes. Laila will be travelling, and will have many responsibilities. School is going to be a challenge in her new role. I wouldn't make any plans based on her schedule. And as to your schooling, you can always contact my office for a reference," Finistere gave Dash a card.

"Yes, thank you." Dash stood up.

"Thank you," the Minister's mind was already somewhere else now that the crisis was over.

"When we were captured by the rebels, they spoke of selling us in the slave markets down in Laayoune."

"There has not been slavery in Morocco for well over a century, more than that, a hundred and fifty years, I think."

"Just because it is not legal doesn't mean it doesn't exist. They just call it different names now. Sex workers, sex trafficking, domestic workers..."

"The disputed territories are a complex issue. And I am not a Minister of the Moroccan government, I only have authority at home."

Dash took off his jacket and tee shirt and threw them on the couch. "May I show you the souvenirs I acquired in the course of our journey?" He then turned his back to the Minister so he could see the scorched and scarred marks on his back from his battle with the scorpion and the burning tar. He'd almost forgotten about his front, but the Minister did not comment.

"Have you seen a doctor? You don't want to risk infection. I can arrange for the Palace doctor to take a look."

"That is not my point, Sir." Dash put his tee shirt back on and then his jacket.

"I appreciate that you risked much for my family, and you will be rewarded. The Prince is grateful." The Minister walked him to the door. "Take your reward, which I believe will be substantial, and start your life somewhere new, far away. Think of your adventure with my daughter as just that, an adventure, of which you will, in time, have fond memories. Your future is not with her. "

"Thank you for your frankness. I shall return the courtesy," Dash's heart was pounding. "The Rebels sell prisoners they don't need in the illegal slave market. I know this because it is all they talk about. You, on the other hand, are selling your own daughter to the Prince. I am having trouble understanding the difference. Am I missing something?

"You are missing something in that you are 16 years old Dash, and you don't know anything."

A minute later Dash was in a long hallway with a guard who walked him to another building with a white painted door that required Dash to stoop to enter. He had been given the room last night and it contained his small duffle bag which held his modest clothing and toiletries.

The guard handed him an envelope. "Be in the courtyard tomorrow morning at 08:00. You are invited to go shooting with the Prince. You will address the Prince as 'Your Highness'. Do not touch his person unless he initiates. Clear?"

"Shooting?"

"Yes, shooting."

"What are we shooting?"

"I was only told shooting, sir."

"Okay..." Dash said thank you and went inside.

Chapter 32

The room Dash had been given was in a building where the temporary staff lived. There was a narrow bed with a cotton mattress stuffed with straw and covered with a stiff sheet, another sheet folded at the foot of it, whitewashed walls, and a ceiling fan. There was a wooden table with a blue ceramic wash basin and jug, a blue towel and a small blue bowl with a few tangerines. He got it, they liked blue around here.

Dash peeled a tangerine aimlessly while staring out the window. He had no idea where to go for food, so he ate the tangerines and admired his new passport. He didn't remember the photograph. Maybe they had taken it at the prison when they had decided to release him. He looked like he needed a meal and a haircut, but then so did most people.

Chapter 33

It was 8 a.m.. Rap music blasted from two Hummers as teenage boys climbed all over them. They were painted in tan and green camouflage and covered with all sorts of gear, whip antennae and netting. A pair of green Land Rovers sat behind with what Dash figured were the Prince's bodyguards.

"You must be Dash," the young man extended his hand. My friends call me 'Abbas'.

"Dashiell Lahlou," Dash said as the young man patted him on the shoulder in greeting.

"We call him "The Lion King", yelled another boy, "because all he does is roar."

"That's Mohamed, watch your back with that one!" The Prince laughed. "You are among friends here. I am in your debt for bringing Laila so safely – to walk through the mountains like that – impressive—do you have a weapon? No?" He turned and signaled to the first Land Rover, and a soldier walked over with an army style vest, a hand gun, goggles and a small shoulder bag of shells and water.

"This is Airsoft. Do you know it?" Abbas asked. "We use the Glock version, we like to get up close and personal."

"You bet," Mohamed had joined them and showed Dash how to load the weapon. "You score points by hitting your man." Mohamed extended his arm.

"Dash has killed two rebels, Mohamed, real ones, and, as legend has it, a giant scorpion. So I don't think you need to show him how to point a gun." Abbas's tone turned serious. "Which is more than you have done, for all your high scores in our games," Abbas turned to Dash. "He is our leading champion, but things change," he grinned while Mohamed ignored him.

"Well, we'll see how you do today, cheb, we work hard for our fun." Mohamed nodded to the Prince and slapped Dash on the shoulder. He had a gold tooth that glinted in the sun. "Ride with me." He gestured to the second Hummer.

Dash looked at the Prince getting into the passenger seat of the first Hummer. "He's not allowed to drive," Mohamed. "It's his great wish, to drive out in the desert and do donuts in the sand. But we do okay."

The Prince was Dash's height, but had ten kilos on him in weight. Dash had dropped weight on their journey. The Prince was handsome and charming, and he was a freaking Prince. He could understand Laila liking him, which made his stomach feel hollow. He liked the Prince too.

"You guys ever ride dirt-bikes?"

"Sure, sometimes we do that. What do you have?"

"Oh, it's old, a Kawasaki, but I take care of it."

"I hope you are around next time we go. Rest a little now, it's going to be hot."

They drove out into the scrub for about an hour. The blasting music did not allow for much conversation, but Mohamed was engaging enough. Dash then fell asleep against the window. When they stopped he stepped out into a surreal landscape centered around an abandoned tank, a half-track, half a dozen blown out adobe buildings and various walls and rubble, with huge sand dunes in the distance.

"Is this real?"

"Algerian war, brother," Mohamed responded. "No fun to fight those fellows. Course I was just a baby." He laughed brightly.

"How does this work?"

"We pick two teams. Yellow and red. Single shot. No bursts when we use assault rifles. You have to shoulder your weapon."

"Sounds fun."

"Yes, you call your shots. Any hit kills. If you are hit you are out, go to your tent, we call it the dead zone." He indicated two shade tents other boys were setting up on the perimeter.

"I'll do my best, it's a lot of rules."

"Don't worry, Abbas loves this stuff. It's how he relaxes."

"Sure."

"Did you really kill rebels? Are you Special Forces?"

"I'm sixteen, a student. It was a weird situation. But yes, I killed. I had no choice."

Chapter 34

The games were so fun and went by so quickly. Everyone was out except Dash and the Prince. Abbas looked very focused. No one was in the tents, everyone circled the boys to see what would happen. They stood about twenty five meters apart. Someone was playing a harmonica.

"Guns at your sides, gentleman," Mohamed called out. "You're free to move around. One shot decides it, like in the old west."

Dash felt sweat on his forehead. What was he supposed to do? He was a guest. He had died in every round, learning the game. He liked the Prince. But he also wanted his respect. He wished he could ask Captain Asim what to do.

The boys circled each other. But in the end this was just shooting, not tactics. Dash knew what to do. The sun was in his eyes but it didn't matter.

Crack.

Assad staggered backwards. A large smile crossed his face and he walked forward to shake Dash's hand and embrace him before the audience had finished gasping. Another boy raised Dash's arm in the air. "Yellow team wins! Time to celebrate!"

Cheers came up but shock was in the air. Dash worried that he had made a mistake. Someone told him that Yellow Team had never won.

Then two of the Royal Guards, their weapons unslung, came over to the Prince. Dash wondered if he was going to be arrested. Then one pointed at the horizon, where a group of dirt bikes were distant silhouettes, stopped, staring at them through binoculars.

"I'm sorry guys! Time to go!" the Prince called out. "Leave the tents."

Everyone stared at the horizon as they stripped their gear and walked towards their vehicles. Dash counted four Royal Guards, plus drivers. They looked calm but concerned.

"Dash, ride with me," the Prince patted Dash on the shoulder.

"Sure."

They were gone in a minute. Dash sat in the back behind behind the Prince. One military Land Rover went first, then the two Hummers, and the second Land Rover, all bumper to bumper, going fast on the paved but ancient road. Dash leaned forward between the front seats to speak to the Prince. He had a bad feeling.

"Your Highness?"

"Yes, Dash?" The Prince smiled. "Don't apologize for killing me. It was great fun. No one has ever had the balls to do it."

"Your Highness, I have a bad feeling. I think we should drive off road, on the left. Those dirt bikes? I think we are being run into a trap up ahead."

The Prince frowned. "I listen to my security detail, but..."

The blast was loud and bright and tremendous. The lead Land Rover was higher in the air than the Hummer, Dash could see its under-carriage as he was thrown back in his seat. Their driver was expert and twisted the twenty-four hundred kilo Hummer into the oncoming lane and onto the shoulder where he braked to a stop.

"Let me out!" Dash yelled. The driver looked at the Prince who nodded. Dash jumped out of the car and yelled "Go!" and slammed his palm against the side of the vehicle. He ran around the bomb crater back to the blown up Land Rover. It was on its side. He pulled open the passenger door. Both Royal Guards were dead. Dash fumbled for their assault rifles and hand guns and jumped down. He couldn't find extra clips. The other Hummer had stopped. Mohamed came running up to him. "What are you doing?"

"Look." Dash pointed at the horizon. The silhouettes of dirt bikes were careening down the dune towards them.

"What do we do?"

"Go! I can slow them down."

"Give me a weapon."

"Go!"

Mohamed ran back to the Hummer, which angled around the blown up Land Rover and the crater and hit the gas. The second Royal Guards Land Rover pulled up and rolled down the window.

"Protect the Prince! Go! Call back-up." The Land Rover took off without a word.

"You should have gone," Dash snapped at Mohamed as he handed him an assault rifle and showed him the safety.

"I love Abbas. He's like my own brother," Mohamed confessed, his voice shaking as they took position behind the truck.

"Then buy time for him to escape. How often do we get to die heroes?"

Mohamed nodded and shouldered his weapon.

These guys could ride, Dash worried as he aimed at the first bike. He didn't have a scope. But he had snake eyes. Thank you Chloe.

Crack! Crack!

Dash dropped the lead biker in a cloud of sand. Mohamed got another with several short, tight bursts. But the four remaining kept coming, only a hundred meters out. They were trained and weaving. Very hard to get a shot. If they got to the road they would be in trouble. Dash handed Mohamed a Glock.

"Stick this in your pants," he yelled, "on your appendix".

"My appendix has been removed."

"Your bad luck," Dash laughed.

Dash lined up his shot. It was terrifying to wait for the right shot, but no choice. Then Dash could see the patterned scarf over the man's mouth. Crack. The man launched backwards off the motorcycle which careened into the air and then crashed in the scrub.

Three left, but they were at the road, Dash's heart was pounding when they veered to the south and headed away from them. Dash ran out into the road, took a knee and pressed the AK into his shoulder as he let off a long burst. Even a tire, he hoped. But they were too fast.

He stood up and he and Mohamed embraced.

"I'll get some water then we'll visit our new friends. Can you work the radio?"

"I'll try"

It was gruesome business climbing in with the dead soldiers. Dash found clips for the rifles, and water as Mohamed tried to work the radio with no luck.

"Just noise" He looked nervously down the road.

They crossed the road and climbed up the dune. Dash's first kill was dead, as was the one Mohamed had nailed. The third one was alive. Mohamed pulled off his helmet and spoke to him in rapid Arabic, but the man did not respond. Mohamed pulled the trigger and his brains splattered all over the sand.

"Don't we need him alive?"

"No," Mohamed sneered. "No, we need him dead."

Dash checked out the crashed dirt bikes. Two of them started, as they had only crashed in sand.

"Can you ride?"

"Shouldn't we wait for support?"

"What if this was a feint, to push the Prince forward? The game site was a defensible location. This highway isn't... can you ride?

"Like a fish, brother."

Dash and Mohamed rode with no helmets, just the Airsoft goggles as the rebel helmets were all smeared inside with blood and brains. So instead they road into the wind, their faces stinging with random sand and insects. Soon enough, in the distance, there was a vertical column of smoke and they went even faster.

Chapter 35

A Land Rover driver was dead in the middle of the road and the windshield was smashed. There were two Royal Guards holding off half a dozen rebel fighters, who were in no hurry, hiding behind rocks and scrub on the other side of the road, trying to pick them off one at a time. The Guards' Land Rover was on the shoulder, smoking from the engine, the friends were scrunched behind it, while the Hummer blocked the road. Dash and Mohamed dropped their bikes.

"Who can ride?"

"I can," a skinny guy named Ahmed from the red team put up his arm.

"Then go!" Dash yelled, then gestured to Mohamed. "Cover him with short bursts – and stay here with the guys."

Mohamed gave him a thumbs up and helped Ahmed with the bike.

Dash knelt beside the Prince, who was leaning back against the rear wheel.

"Are you hit?" Dash pulled off his own body armor.

"No, how are we doing?"

"We are kicking ass. Wear this." Dash helped with the armor. "Stay here."

Dash fired a short burst across the road and crouched beside one of the Royal Guards. "Have you been able to call it in?"

"Not sure. Radio took a bullet. I'm Sami and this is Rahman, like the soup."

Rahman yelled. "Can you believe, this is the first time I hear this joke?"

"I am Dash, how are you guys for ammo?"

"There's gear in the truck, but we're kind of stuck here."

"I'll go. Then I'm going to take the orange bike and circle around behind them. Don't shoot me. Mohamed will stay with the guys. We sent Ahmed on the other bike to get help."

"Roger that."

"You got any grenades?"

"Back of the Rover."

Dash found several grenades in a box with foam cutouts. Fancy. Bullets whistled overhead. And a box of ammo. He stuffed two clips in his pants and carried the box holding the rest to the Royal Guards.

"How do these grenades work?"

Sami put down his weapon and showed him. "Don't put one down your pants by mistake."

"Right. You'll know when I make my move. You come too."

"We're supposed to stay with the Prince."

"Okay, okay, I'll figure it out. Good luck."

Dash lifted the last dirt bike and slung his weapon over his shoulder. It was not comfortable for what he had to. He heard heavier firing. Ahmed must have taken off north. Dash spun his rear tire and headed south. As soon as he was out of eyesight he crossed the shoulder and headed up into the scrub and the dunes. He wanted to surprise them from height.

He hid behind the crest of a dune and surveyed the scene. Sporadic fire from both sides, half a dozen rebels. Half a dozen dirt bikes right behind him, grouped together. The rebels wanted the Prince alive for ransom. All they had to do was wait until his guards ran out of ammo. They had no support truck, but perhaps they figured they would capture a vehicle.

Dash loved dirt-bikes, since he was a kid. He did not want to do this. He peeled off his shirt and opened the fuel tank on one, soaking the shirt. He piled the bikes on top of each other. It hurt him to do it. He got back on his bike, pulled out the Glock so he could aim while riding, and pulled the pin on one of the grenades. This was going to piss off the rebels big time. He was going to burn their rides.

He revved his engine, then lobbed the grenade into the middle of the bikes. The blast almost blew him over as he scrambled over the hill towards the scrub where the rebels were positioned. A few of them stood up, staring back at the fireball in the sky. Dash wondered if they even saw him. He turned hard and spun to south side of the scrub as he saw the two Royal Guards step out and take aim as they crossed the road.

Crack.

Crack.

Crack.

Crack.

Crack.

It looked like Rahman who took a bullet to the thigh but kept shooting. Dash stopped the bike, took the AK and sprayed the rebel line with the entire clip.

It was over.

Sami and Dash dragged the bodies to the shoulder and lined them up in a row. One of the boys took pictures of their faces. It would be a long day of debriefing tomorrow.

Above them the sky was still full of smoke. It was a fine signal marker for when the rescue squad showed up. Sami and Dash then put the wounded Rahman in the back of the Hummer after stopping the bleeding in his leg. They could barely squeeze in. Dash and Mohamed embraced.

"Your Highness – wanna drive?" Dash handed him the keys and climbed on somebody's lap. Sami climbed in the front and tried to get the radio to work

"Are you sure you want to drive, your Highness." Sami asked.

"Yes, I am sure." the Prince grinned and hit the gas, making the tires screech and the took off into the scrub.

Ten minutes of careening along and they saw the choppers and the Prince braked. The helicopters landed in a vast cloud of dust.

Chapter 36

There is regular fear, and then there is the fear of dying in a helicopter. Dash clung to his seat and closed his eyes. Then he peeked at Mohamed, who was smoking a cigarette and laughing. Maybe he had done this before.

He looked behind him at the five body bags. Two Royal Guards and the three Rebels.

"Don't throw up!" Mohamed admonished him. "You should see your face, man!"

Finally they landed. At least Captain Asim was there. He embraced the boys and handed them off to another officer. "I have to…"

"I understand. Is the Prince safe?"

"Yes. He is in the other chopper, with Rahman and Sami. What happened?"

"They came out of the sand, six of them that we saw."

"Kidnapping or murder?"

"We never saw a support vehicle, but maybe they thought they'd get one of ours."

"This is very bad."

"Then we sent the Prince ahead, but there was a second ambush. Mohamed here got at least a pair, he was the hero," Dash said, beginning to understand the politics.

"Tell the investigating officers everything. You boys did great."

They were taken into a private lounge at the military airport and given bottles of Coke and told to wait.

"Are you wounded. Do either of you need medical attention?" A corporal asked.

"No, I'm good. Mohamed? Are you good?"

"Never been better, could we get a deck of cards?"

"I'll check," the corporal disappeared.

"Cards?" Dash frowned.

"This is going to take a while. We can sleep or play cards – or we can talk about what bad-asses we were today. Or are you the modest type?"

Dash raised his bottle and clinked it against Mohamed's. "Salut. I was glad to have you beside me."

"I was glad to have me beside you too," Mohamed struggled to light a cigarette. "About what I said…"

"What?"

"The part about loving Abbas? I wasn't planning on putting it in this report. You weren't thinking of including it, were you?"

"No, no, it's unnecessary detail, I think. We were just doing what we could, you know, under the circumstances."

"Good. Anyway, the story is simple."

"Yeah, yeah. Simple."

"Good."

"Simple is good."

The corporal returned with more drinks and the deck of cards.

Mohamed grinned and shuffled the deck. "Basra? Poker?"

"Sure."

"You have money to lose?"

"Not a centime.

Chapter 37

Dash returned to his room very late, showered and slept. In the morning he told the stories of the Café Comedie and the Airsoft battle again to different security teams, but they were respectful and interested and they fed him.

Late in the day he tried to call Laila to no avail, so he slept for an hour and then a guard came and escorted him to the dinner in honor of he and Mohamed.

Though he was excited about the dinner and to see everyone, he felt a malaise pressing on his chest. Perhaps just weariness from the long journey, perhaps the realization that each time he saw Laila might be the last. Maybe heartache. He knew he was becoming a man now and this was probably normal, but it sucked whatever paint you put on it.

The banquet room was beautiful. The fragrant food calmed him. Rack of lamb with eggplant and fig puree, grilled poussin, grilled fish dishes – tables were laden with every delicacy, and many flowers. The Prince had gone to a lot of trouble. There were maybe forty people at the dinner. Dash was seated with Mohamed and the Prince's other personal friends, mostly from the Airsoft event. Laila came in last, in a turquoise dress sewn with delicate orange flowers, she sat with the Prince and her father and Captain Asim.

The Prince impressed Dash with his charm, he engaged everyone and made them comfortable. He gave Dash a canvas belt with pockets full of small gold bars. It was far heavier than it looked. The time came for Dash to speak, Captain Asim had introduced him. He felt light-headed as he got up and went to the podium with the microphone where the Prince was waiting.

"Thank you. I never expected an honor like this in my life. Well, maybe at the end, if things go well... but I am only sixteen and can only hope this is not the high point."

That got a big laugh and the Prince put his arm on Dash's shoulder.

"I only did what was necessary for my friends, and I would do it again tomorrow. I am blessed that God put me in a position to help. Thank you."

Dash dared not look at Laila as he returned to his chair. Mohamed also got up to receive an award from the Prince.

"This is great, your Highness. Thank you. Now I can afford to hang out with you." They embraced, obviously they were close.

Dash admired how relaxed the boys were, joking even in the aftermath of the attack. He liked the Prince and Mohamed so much. Everyone was mingling now and Laila finally came and knelt beside his chair.

"Are you going?"

"Tonight."

"Who will take care of me?"

"Your Prince, it's his job, isn't it?"

"Don't be bitter."

"Plus Asim, the Royal Guards... I will return as soon as I get my parents settled. You are much loved, Laila, everyone will watch out for you."

"We can still go to school together?"

"Yes, our great plan..." Dash laughed, thinking sadly of her father's words.

"Dash, I was always happy to do what my father wanted," Laila dropped her voice to a whisper. "But... all this... you know all the important and great things they want me to do... sometimes I wish we could go to America together. I could hide you in my dorm room, we could go on a luxury ocean liner, like in the old days."

"Yeah, like that movie, the Titanic."

"Am I so foolish to want my own life?"

"I want you to..."

"Dash!" The Prince helped Laila to her feet and clapped Dash on the shoulder, as did Mohamed. "We've upgraded your award. Each year we are going to hold an Airsoft event and give out the "Dash" award for the best shooter."

"And the trophy will be a small motorcycle helmet on a stand," Mohamed added, cracking himself up. "With blood splattered on the inside."

"I'm glad you are amusing yourselves," Dash said as he stood.

"Please, let us see you soon. Next time we'll do dirt bikes. Come out on the balcony with us for a smoke."

"Sure, sure..."

Laila took the Prince's arm. As she walked away her father came over and shook Dash's hand warmly. "Beautiful couple, don't you think?"

"Yes, of course, Sir."

"Congratulations on your award. So what are your plans, Dash?"

"The same, I'm going to Tangier on the midnight train, I will meet up with my parents, and prepare to write my exams."

The Minister leaned forward and whispered. "If you stay in Morocco, you should spend your money quickly."

Chapter 38

After the party Dash was alone in his room, packing his meager belongings, admiring his new passport. There was a sharp rap at the door.

"Captain Asim, come in."

There was one wooden chair. Dash sat on the bed with his knees up as Asim sat on the chair, twisting his red beret in his hands.

"You are leaving tonight?"

"Yes," Dash shrugged. "I can come back if the Security Service need me again. Have an orange. Somehow they taste bitter."

"What do you know about ducks?"

"Ducks?"

"Their feet are always moving under the water. That is what politics are like. My investigation into the Café killers has been closed. I've already been given another assignment – supposedly because the attack on the Prince." Asim finally put down his beret and began peeling the mandarin."You are very young, Dash. I had hopes of recruiting you to the Royal Guards, the Prince supports the idea, but our bureaucracy will not hear of it because you are not a citizen."

"Laila is not a citizen either, though I guess she will become one by marriage."

"Laila should not have praised you so highly in front her father- and neither should I have praised you, though how could I not? You might have saved the Prince's life with your calm and tactically sound actions. You have a gift."

Asim reached into his jacket pocket and pulled out a gun. From the other pocket a box of cartridges. He set them on the table and stood up.

"I don't want you travelling without protection. Dash, we have only known each other a short time, but you have won my friendship with your courage."

Dash stood up also.

"The King," Asim continued, "whom I have served for ten years, is now old. His health is deteriorating quickly. He is not really in Sweden, as they announced at dinner to explain his absence. He is in a clinic in Switzerland. The rebels have friends, they have many spies in the palace. When the King dies, a fake coup d'état will be attempted, in the name of getting rid of royalty, more democracy, which of course will be a lie. The Prince will be paraded as the hero, but the truth is that the rebels will become the power behind the throne, and the Prince will become a cardboard King. It is not his fault. He is not experienced in politics. For our people, there will be nothing but suffering."

"You are giving me a headache."

"Laila is the prize, as the bride of the Prince she will be the face of peace, to save thousands of lives. The price may also be our young democracy, but the alternative is too horrible. Asim's eyes stared at the floor. This story is only what I think... my opinion. If I could prove it, I would be already dead."

"Where will you be?"

"I am being sent to the south, to make a soft probe of rebel strength, in the hope that I will be killed, probably by one of my squad, who will be paid for that result. I am too loyal to the King and the monarchy.

"I wish we could fight together."

"You have the taste for blood now?" Asim frowned.

"No. I have a taste for freedom. Finistere gave me the kiss of death tonight at the end of the dinner. He said to leave Morocco or spend my money quickly."

"He has profound influence at court, even after the death of his brother. I cannot understand. Come to the back service gate in 30 minutes I will drive you to the train.

"I'd hoped to say good-bye to Laila."

"Dash, her father's men might come at any time. The Minister will do anything to make sure the marriage to the Prince goes ahead."

"I thought the Prince wanted to be friends."

"He does, but he does not understand the danger of this arrangement. They want to align the policies of Algeria and Morocco with respect to the southern territories. They need the marriage to sell it."

Dash's eyes darkened, like an imminent storm and he found the strength to stand up. He and Asim embraced.

"Gattopardo," Dash realized. "We can keep in touch through him."

"He is not too corrupt?"

"He has quite a sense of dignity, actually... how funny is that?" Dash laughed.

"It was one thing to go along with the plan for Laila to marry the Prince and be a sign to the people, when it was an abstract idea," Asim continued, knowing he had much to say and not much time in which to say it. "Now, that I have met her... but there is nothing we can do, I am sorry."

"What will happen now?"

"We will try to stay alive, to be of service to the King while he lives, to the Prince if we can, and for Laila, who will need her friends more than ever in the coming storm."

Chapter 39

After Asim dropped him at the station, Dash did not get on the next train that ran from Rabat to Tangier. He trusted Asim, but he wanted to make sure Laila did not need him. The truth was he could not bring himself to leave.

He slept in student/backpacker places around the University for a few days, never the same place twice, sleeping hard on the roofs, where it would be difficult to surprise him and where he was more comfortable anyway. He knew the train station was watched, and he needed time to think.

Each day he called Gattopardo at an agreed time. On the second day he was told to go to a certain café. The elderly man who owned it had been described to him.

They went into a back room and sat at a kitchen table. The man showed him how to disassemble and clean and reload the gun Asim had given him. Over and over, until finally he could do it blind-folded.

The man refused payment, saying that he was a friend of Gattopardo, and being able to repay such a favor was far more valuable than money. Gattopardo was apparently not a man to whom you wanted to be obligated.

Dash ate well and slept. His body had taken such a beating it was necessary, especially his feet needed time to heal. And the killings. They played in his head and often he would wake up in the night panting and full of anxiety.

Finally, at the end of each day, he would go to a crowded internet café and read every story about Laila and the Prince, of which there were many. She wore a hijab to cover her bandaged ear. Laila at the local hospital comforting children. Laila and the Prince welcoming guests at the palace. Already they were speaking of her resemblance to Dihya Kahina, the warrior princess.

But after only a few days, the girl in the articles seemed to be changing from the Laila that Dash knew into someone else. Finally his phone rang.

"Are you okay?"

"Sure. Letting my body heal for a few days." Dash felt the stress leave his body.

"You haven't left?"

"Just hanging out, hoping you would call and tell me how happy you are."

"Oh Dash... it's impossible."

"Maybe I'm just moping around, hoping you will walk away from it all."

"Dash you have an obligation to your parents, I understand. You have to understand my family situation. Go and deal with your family."

"Call Gatto for my numbers. I'm going to be using burner phones from now on.

"Oh Dash, what kind of phone is that?"

"You get a new one each day."

"That makes no sense."

"Laila, did your father ask you about my plans?"

"Sure. I just said you wanted to be a doctor. And to go to school here in Rabat. You can afford it now anyway."

"Someone betrayed us at the Café Comedie. Don't share any plans we make with anyone. Not even your father or the Prince."

"I understand... by the way all Abbas and Mohamed do is talk about you. I think they'd rather have you around than me."

Dash laughed.

"And you owe me some pretty ear rings."

"Yes."

Chapter 40

The train was going to Tangier which sat on both the Atlantic and Mediterranean coasts across from Gibraltar.

The train was full and slow, the cars rocked and groaned. But Dash had a window seat, his stomach was full, he could feel the weight of the gold around his waist. Most importantly he didn't have to walk. His feet still hurt and the gold was heavy. He folded his jacket for a pillow and kept his duffel bag in his lap, his arm through a strap, and his hand on his gun just inside the bag.

Rebels had apparently attacked a train the previous week, though not on this route, but Dash was more concerned about casual thieves if he fell asleep. In fact he badly needed to sleep, and let the motion and his bittersweet thoughts of Laila help him drift away.

Thunk. Thunk. Thunk. Dash awoke but did not open his eyes. Slowly his brain began to work, and he reluctantly looked through his eyelashes at the bench directly across from him. The old women were gone. Placeholders. Two men had replaced them. Nasty looking thugs. Mid-twenties, tough looking, dressed casually liked they lived in a city. But the snake venom in his blood told him that they were killers.

Dash made a snoring sound and moved slightly, positioning his body. He could see out the window now by barely opening his eyes.. Was there another stop before they reach the tunnel. The famous tunnel. That's where they would kill him. With knives. It would be pitch black and the sound of the train would echo. One would cover Dash's mouth while pushing his chin up with his open hand and pin Dash's knees with his own. The second man would slit his throat, like a goat, or if the angle was bad, stab him through the ribs, hoping to hit a lung or his heart. They would have practiced it. They would cut off the gold belt and be gone to the next train car. The famous tunnel took nearly two minutes. Plenty of time. There were no soldiers on this train, at least not this car. Women, children and old men, mostly sleeping.

It would suddenly become very loud and dark when they entered the tunnel. Dash knew what to do. He kept his eyes closed. It would be an advantage if his eyes were already used to the darkness. He ever so slowly let the safety off his gun. He doubted he would even have time to pull the gun out of his bag.

His Adidas duffel bag that he was so proud of was going to have holes in it. He just knew they would wait for the tunnel. Part of him felt sad. Everything he and Laila had been through in the mountains, being chased by the rebels, the café killers. They had survived by being clever. Throwing the old bullets in the fire. The help from Ferrous the Bear and Cleo the Asp. Was the purpose of all this just for him to die with his throat slit on a train? At least he had done what he had promised to Laila's father. Delivered her safely to Uncle Taha. The bitter irony of that was not lost on him.

He waited. Every nerve on end. Then, suddenly, the train slowed a little as they headed uphill and into the tunnel. Pitch black and very loud. The train was swaying from side to side. Dash opened his eyes as the man directly across from him stood up. He had to use one hand to balance against the window and reached forward with the other. Dash fired.

Crack.

Dash heard pain and shock, as if from far away. Then Dash twisted his wrist just slightly and fired again.

Crack.

The second man kept coming. Dash felt a searing pain in his left arm.

Crack. The second man fell on top of Dash. It took all Dash's strength to push him back to his seat. Dash could see well enough in the dark. The first man was slumped back in his seat, with both hands covering his groin. Dash took the butt of his weapon and smacked it hard against the man's jaw. Now the man would neither be able to talk or piss. That was even better than killing him. The other fellow was quite dead.

Dash was not cruel, but he was done. Done with being chased and threatened for nothing. He had not asked for any of this. He pulled out one of his new tee shirts and tied it around his left bicep. The knife wound hurt like hell but it was not deep. Just bloody.

He positioned the two men to look like they were sleeping. At the next town he would just get off the train and disappear.

Dash is worried about Laila changing, but it seems that he is changing too. They have been through so much, and now they are separated. It appears that Laila is safe, surrounded by security, but is she really? I stared at Laila's hair, which she has now tied into a pony-tail. For the first time I am afraid she might be beyond where Dash can help her, and Dash has his own problems. I have to be vigilant here and keep my eye on her, but right now Dash is in trouble.

Chapter 41

Dash stumbled off the train and wandered through the medina, feeling faint, until he came to a fountain. He knelt on the stone steps and cupped water into his hands and splashed his face, then drank and drank, though it was not wise to drink fountain water. It seemed impossible to drink enough. His breathing was shallow. His sleeve was soggy with blood under the tied tee-shirt.

He saw an attractive older American-looking woman, maybe 30.

Staring at him. He thought she might be American because a few tendrils of blonde hair protruded from her head scarf. He felt faint as he tried to stand, but it wasn't possible. His whole arm and shoulder had gone numb. Suddenly he knew. There had been poison on the knife blade. That was the last thing he remembered.

Chapter 42

In fact it was Dash's modern western clothes that caught Heather's attention, because his wardrobe was so incongruous with his face, a face that was both young and ancient, beautiful yet fierce. She could not imagine him as a typical teenager, in sneakers and a football team polo. She watched as he collapsed on the fountain steps, and when he didn't move she went to check on him. That was just her personality. She hoped he wasn't overdosing on drugs or something equally stupid. Then she saw his blood soaked sleeve.

The boy's eyes were rolled back in his head and he had a terrible fever. She looked around for a police officer or someone to help, but there were only women and elderly men weaving in and out of the market. She could take the boy to her flat, which anyway was only around the corner, and telephone Freddy the English doctor. She managed to get Dash upright, and they stumbled over the cobblestones as he moaned.

Luckily she had a ground floor flat, and a long wooden bench with beautiful woven cushions on it beside the large open kitchen she had had built for her work. She stripped the cushions, got Dash on it and began to boil water. She untied the tee shirt and looked at the long wound, it was still bleeding and the blood did not seem to be coagulating.

She called her doctor friend but he didn't pick up, so she left a message. She knew she needed to put pressure on the wound, but she didn't have anything more than band aids. She did, however, have gauzy cheese cloth, used for straining foods or making little bags of herbs. Inspired, she took a clean sponge and gently washed the wound and wrapped it tightly with the cheese cloth, and then a clean kitchen towel. She stared at Dash with curiosity - he was so young. She had the ironic thought that chefs - like herself - sometimes used blood instead of flour to thicken a sauce. Maybe she should use flour to thicken this boy's blood?

Next she soaked another towel in cold water and put it on his forehead. That was it. When he woke up she could give him Tylenol. Like most American travelers, she had a full complement of over-the-counter medicines. There was nothing more to do until Freddy dropped by. Not that he had a real practice here. He had assorted word-of-mouth patients, mostly expat Americans and Europeans, but his main work was at the local hospital, where he had a teaching position.

She lifted Dash's duffel bag off the floor and put it on the end of the couch. It was awfully heavy and clunky at one end. She unzipped it and looked, she couldn't help herself, maybe there was some I.D. so she could at least learn his name. Folded clothes, a few toiletry items—and a gun. She froze, re-zipping the bag as quietly as she could.

"I would have looked too."

Heather's heart pounded as her head spun to see Dash's weak smile.

Dash tried to sit up, leaning on his good elbow. Perhaps she should have been scared, but his eyes were soft and sad, not aggressive at all.

"You don't look like..." Heather's heart was pounding.

"I didn't think so either."

"Are you a rebel?"

"Dash's eyes clouded over. "A long time ago I could have killed some of them, but I didn't, because some of them are younger than me... thank you... Miss... I remember seeing you in the medina. Thank you... no... I am no rebel."

"I rang a doctor friend," was all she could manage. "Take these, for your fever."

Dash obediently swallowed the Tylenol and glugged half a bottle of mineral water.

"Your wound is... unusual, or rather, it's not a bad enough cut to make you unconscious and fevered. I'm a chef, I've seen plenty of knife wounds." She leaned over and put her palm on his forehead. He was still very hot and his breathing was labored. She had a meat thermometer in the kitchen. Maybe she should get that.

"I was poisoned, by a knife," Dash shrugged casually as he swung his legs around and put his feet on the floor. "You're an American."

"Yes," my name is Heather Burroughs. "I'm a chef in New York. I'm on a sabbatical learning Moroccan cooking and I post a blog from this kitchen. What's your name."

"Dash. Dash Lahlou."

"Your English is excellent," Heather continued. "I thought kids here studied French?"

Dash frowned. His English was a gift from Cleo. He probably wasn't going to explain that. At least he could understand this pretty lady and knew what to say back to her.

"Thank you. I am so grateful. But I need to go."

"You're in no condition to go anywhere."

"Police will come. Soldiers will come. There will be trouble for you if you help me more than you already have."

"At least see the doctor," she continued. "He's a good friend, I'm sure he'll come by."

"I don't think I should have any new medicine put in my blood..." Dash didn't know how to explain. "There is the poison in my blood, and medicine... yes, that's what it is... medicine... that is already there. The poison and the medicine are fighting inside of me. I can feel it. No one can interfere or... I have to go to Tangier." Dash stood, and immediately staggered, saving himself by leaning on the kitchen island and laughed weakly. "My eyes are blurry,"

"What did you do, that the police would search the medina?"

"Are they?"

"I don't know. I heard whistles in the distance."

"I was on the train to Tangier. Men tried to kill me. I had to kill them. Two... men..."

"You could explain that," Heather tried to sound helpful and not frightened.

"Then I will be killed in the jail... I don't want you to get in trouble."

"At least eat something. I'm making beghir - at least I'm trying to make it. You can tell me if it's any good."

"You should come to my village," he grinned. "Grandma will teach you anything you wish." Dash sighed at the thought of home.

"The police know me, I'm the crazy American who asks too many questions. They would never imagine to look for you here. And Freddy speaks the lingo fluently, he'll handle them."

Heather's argument was wasted, for Dash had slumped to the floor and was again asleep.

Chapter 43

It was the next day and the worst had not happened. Doctor Freddy had come, stayed for a drink and to stitch the wound, then drawn some blood from the unconscious Dash and taken it back to the hospital. He was in love with Heather and would do anything to help her, but they had to wait on the blood test results.

"Thank you Doctor, but no shot, please," Dash sat up again on both elbows, his face damp and flushed, his eyes unfocused.

"Were you ever bitten by a cobra before, son? My only thought is that you - you look like a Berber - may have evolved some degree of natural immunity - though I have never heard of such a thing."

"Snakes no. Scorpions yes. They are nasty - may I go doctor? It's not safe for you or Miss Heather if I am here."

"Dash, you are awfully brave, but you couldn't walk to the door. Let me check you into the hospital and I can at least get you on intravenous for hydration and to get your fever down."

Dash stood up and immediately felt dizzy.

"Freddie!" Heather grabbed him. "Help me get him in my bed."

The next morning Heather came out of the shower and put on coffee. She liked to go out early before the heat, but Freddy was already tapping on the door. He was wearing a bright Hawaiian shirt.

"I wanted to come right away. Is your house guest alive?"

"Yes, I am certain because he snores," Heather laughed as she made coffee.

"You slept with him?" Freddy looked stunned.

"Freddy, I have one bed, and he's just a boy."

Freddy got a stormy look on his face.

"Freddy, he's a kid. Anyway, it's not like you and I exclusive."

"What's that supposed to mean?"

"Oh, it means you haven't had your coffee yet."

Freddie pulled a folded sheet of paper on his pocket and leaned on the kitchen island staring at it while he sipped his coffee. Heather went in the other room to get dressed.

"He's been bitten by a snake, Heather," Freddy called out. "An asp. Member of the cobra family. Snakes that killed Cleopatra. He has enough venom in him to kill someone weighing a hundred kilos!"

Heather came back into the room, dressed, and wearing a shocked look.

"Plus some other kind of poison made from local scorpions, I could have the lab break it down further, but... my point is he shouldn't be walking. He should be dead. When I examined him I found the punctures on his leg, one bite, but I couldn't find a puncture from a scorpion, so maybe the knife wound. Would explain why the blood was so slow to coagulate. And he's got those damn strange scabs on his chest, and his back has burn marks – these are all very recent wounds, not sure what this boy does in his spare time."

"Yes," Heather nodded as she stirred her own coffee and watched Freddy in a curious way. "The wounds are impressive."

"Recent. But no infection. We have snake anti-venom, but the anti-scorpion venom they use here doesn't really work. He needs to be in the hospital."

"He doesn't want any anti-venom. He was most insistent about it."

"He should be dead... the toxins in his system... the level is fascinating. You need to let me put him in the hospital. Just for observation. Here I can't help him."

"Tomorrow, Freddy. Tomorrow."

Dash slept all day and ate some food in the afternoon. That night he again shared Heather's bed. But Freddy came back after his evening rounds. The front door was never locked, and he saw Dash still in Heather's bed. He left quietly but on fire with jealous rage.

Chapter 44

Dash woke in a white-washed room he didn't remember entering. An intravenous drip had been inserted into his arm with a clear liquid in the bag.

More curiously, many different sensors were taped to his chest and forehead and different machines beeped and clucked beside the bed. At least his arm had been properly bandaged. The last thing he remembered was Heather's dreamy scent of flour and perfume.

Voices murmured in the next room, but Dash could not distinguish the words. He sat up. The dizziness faded a little. He unplugged the sensors and the I.V. then stood and quietly eased over by the door until he could hear Dr. Freddy.

"Okay, keep him sedated. The police will pick him up in an hour. They think he's the one who killed those fellows on the train. I'll be back before they get here."

Dash frowned. What was Freddy's problem? He gazed the room for his clothes, at least they were there, in a small closet. Hopefully Heather still had his Adidas bag. The screens beeped and blinked but it meant nothing to him. He could walk. He angled to the door. A male attendant sat at a small desk typing at a computer. It was an outer office then there was a door to a hallway.

"I have no plans to hurt you, but..."

"How are *you* walking?" The attendant, even though he was bigger than Dash, just stared.

"I've had better days," Dash reached for a roll of white medical tape. "Put your wrists on the arms of the chair."

The attendant did that, though he didn't much like it. Dash taped his arms to the chair and then taped his mouth shut.

"Sorry, nothing personal. Can you breathe?"

The man nodded.

Dash changed into his street clothes. He closed the door softly behind him and took the stairs down to the lobby and out into the street. There was no panic behind him. The trouble was he had no idea where he was.

Dash recognized the Hawaiian shirt. Freddy.

Freddy's pissed off face.

Freddy pointing at him.

Two officers grabbed Dash's elbows from behind. A practiced rabbit punch in the kidney, Dash's knees bent, handcuffs. Freddy got in Dash's face and wildly punched at his jaw, hitting his shoulder. The third cop tried to restrain Freddy.

Dash laughed.

"Okay, show's over," said one cop to the quickly gathering crowd. They threw Dash in the side door of the white police mini-van. There was one bench seat, seat belts just a memory. The cops sat in the front. The driver started to maneuver patiently through the crush of traffic.

The front cop turned and gave Dash the once over. "He's just a kid! Doesn't look like a 'Tchermil'." He frowned and turned his round face towards Dash. "I'm Officer Karim, he's Officer Simo. But I have seniority."

Simo laughed, "One year seniority, and you think you are king of the jungle."

"Are you going to start with me? We have just captured a dangerous fugitive. Killed two armed men on a train, not that I'm buyin' that story."

"I thought one of them might live," Dash mumbled.

Both officers stared at Dash.

"You can't say that man!"

"Cause then we gotta write it down."

"Yeah, and then somebody's going to read it and ask questions we can't answer."

Dash closed his eyes. He wished they would let him sleep.

"Shouldn't you be writing this shit down?" Simo started. "Seein' as you have senior…

"Those men are the train were trying to rob me, and kill me, the killing part was supposed to come first, I guess."

"Did you know them?" Karim was searching his pockets for a pencil.

"You really dangerous?" Simo twisted in his seat and frowned.

"I haven't even passed my bacca yet. How dangerous can I be?"

Simo nodded as he considered that answer. Neither he or Karim had even stood for that test.

"We hand off this young fellow fast, Simo," Karim announced. "*Tchermil* street punks don't walk around in western suits. Something else is going on here that we don't want to know."

Simo opened his mouth to argue, but before a word could be chosen there was a white flash through the windows, like a giant flashbulb, which Dash saw as he was straining his neck seeking some landmark by which to orient himself so that if he were able to escape he would know how to get back to Heather's house and get his gun and money belt. Then came a deafening roar and a hot blast they felt through the metal walls of the van. The blast blew out the side windows, pelting them with pebbles of glass. The van was pushed on its side and the back doors burst. Simo ended up in the back seat under Dash, then Karim crawled into the back and pulled Dash off of him.

Karim then crawled out the back door on his hands and knees. The bench seat was broken off its rails.

Dash heard staccato gun fire and saw Karim reach for his side arm but blood splashed out from the exit wound on his back on to the inside of the rear door. Two robed men dragged him into the middle of the square where a third man was firing random bursts. Dash and Simo must have looked plenty dead.

Dash crawled up beside Simo, who was now shaking.

"Where are you hurt?"

"Leg."

Simo's leg was twisted weirdly underneath him. Dash helped him move his pelvis to make him more comfortable.

"Is that better."

"Yeah, but I think it is broken."

"I'm going to take your gun," Dash whispered urgently. "Is that okay?"

Simo nodded and rolled on his hip. Dash pulled the gun.

"Kid there are clips in the glove box and a .38 revolver. Get that for me."

Dash did that and then lay flat on what was the side of the van. It was not easy to manoeuver wearing handcuffs. "

"The key is on my belt," Simo offered, reading Dash's mind, "for the handcuffs. Can we help Karim first? He is from my village, and it would really piss him off to die this way."

"We can do it... Simo, can you handle your weapon? Can you cover me without hitting Karim?"

Dash backed up and helped Simo with the .38. They lay flat on their stomachs in the pebbled glass. The first two rebels now had Karim on his knees as they dragged him forward, blood stained the stones behind him. The third rebel shouldered his weapon and pulled out his cell phone. Sirens howled in the distance under screams and cries.

"Looks like they are going to make a speech, then execute Karim and video it."

"We have to do something."

"On my signal."

Dash tried to make his eyes focus as the first rebel put his gun to Karim's head and began screaming some sort of manifesto.

"Legs! Hit their legs!" Dash yelled at Simo, thinking that it's not that easy to get information out of dead people.

Crack.

Crack.

Crack.

Crack.

Crack.

Dash fired until the gun was empty and lay his head on the ground. "Thank you Cleo," he whispered.

Their bullets had ripped through the three men and they lay where they fell.

Dash got up and kicked their guns away. Their eyes were crazy. One of them was wearing a suicide vest stuffed with red squares which must have been the explosive. Dash picked up the man's assault rifle and anger rushed through him, he didn't know how to disarm a suicide bomber.

Crack.

The black hole in the man's forehead was a punctuation mark that solved the problem. There was nothing to say. That left two of them alive to question. The sirens got louder. Dash wanted so badly to run, but somehow he was just so weary. He did not know what Doctor Freddy had done to him.

"Don't touch them, there is a bomb vest! Get back!"

That backed the crowd off. Karim was still on his knees, head bent, traumatized, still waiting to be shot.

"Let me help you, Officer." Dash put his shoulder under the man's arm. He could not tell how bad the wounds were but at least one shot had entered his chest. The sirens were getting louder. Several of the onlookers were videoing Dash and the officer as they slumped on the steps of a small fountain. Dash took off his own shirt and pressed it into the wound.

"Can you keep pressure on?"

Officer Karim just nodded. Someone offered a bottle of water, and helped him to drink.

Dash looked around for the first time to see where the bomb had gone off, the blast that had knocked over the van in the first place.

A café. Les Perdrix Blanc. Dozens of people milled around, many were laying on the ground. Windows were broken, tables knocked over. A car still burned, dark smells of fuel and rubber and other things Dash did not know. Probably the bomb car. The typical rebel plan would have been to detonate the bomb car first, and then the three rebels would have hit the first wave of police and medical response, finishing off with the suicide vest.

That was how previous attacks had worked, it had just been bad luck that their police van had driven by at that moment.

The first ambulance and police cars were arriving now.

Dash walked back to check on Simo.

"They told us you were dangerous," Simo yelled in his ear, both still deaf from the blast.

Dash's head was pounding.

"Why aren't you getting away?" Simo continued. "I told you, the keys to the cuffs are on my belt."

"You guys will get in trouble if I go. Anyway, I'm tired."

"Trouble? We just got this van! We were walkin' a month ago! We're going to be walking again! If we still have jobs," Simo decided.

Dash led a medic to Karim. Dash stared at his handcuffed wrists. It would be a while until they got to him. Maybe he would take a nap. He lay back on the stones and felt the warm sun on his face.

"Wake up asshole," a new cop yelled as he kicked Dash. Dash sat up. There were a lot of cops now, with fancy SWAT gear, running around like that was helping. Dash held his hands out in front of him so they could see his jewelry. Just once he'd like to wake up in peace and quiet. Birds chirping, the warm sun on his face. Just once.

Chapter 45

Dash was in the bottom of a cone-shaped well that narrowed towards the top, maybe only ten meters up with one arched window, just enough to tell day from night. The bars were old, the stones were round and ancient. Dash lay on the floor, appreciating the coolness. He was wearing his pants and a plain tee shirt someone must have given him. No bed, no table, no chair. He was alone in the cell, which was unusual. Moroccan prisons were notorious for over-crowding.

On the 2nd day a sullen guard brought him a bowl of boiled vegetables and stale bread.

"I had no food yesterday."

"If I had brought food yesterday, you would not have eaten it. Then both the food, and the journey to bring it would have been wasted."

Dash nodded at this relentless logic. "What is your name?"

"Sajjan the Jailor. It is sufficient for you."

"Okay, Sajjan the Jailor, are there any books?"

"No one has ever asked for one."

Sajjan the Jailor shuffled away. Dash ate the food and realized Sajjan had been right. Yesterday he would not have eaten it.

On the 4th day, Sajjan brought an old Mexican wrestling magazine.

"Yesterday I had no magazine."

"Yesterday you would not have read it."

"You are right, of course. Thank you."

On the 7th day a new man came, in traditional clothing, bright birds' eyes and an impressive silver beard.

"I am Azima, your advocate."

"Yesterday I had no advocate," Dash slumped against the wall.

"Everyone says that," Azim grinned and looked up. "I have been coming to this prison for twenty years, yet I have never seen this cell."

Dash closed his magazine and put it on the floor.

"So today is worthwhile for you?"

"At my age, each day is worthwhile, especially when it brings something new."

"Come, they have prepared a room for us," Azim gestured with his hand.

Sajjan blindfolded Dash and they walked slowly. "So, Advocate, you have a new customer?"

"Yes. I hope he has not been difficult."

"He needs his bandages changed."

"I will make the arrangements."

"Thank you."

"So, Dash Lahlou," the advocate began, how have you been treated here?"

"Thank you for asking. No one has talked to me about my case, neither have I been beaten or hung like a bled-out chicken."

"Because I have just been appointed, and because the outside investigation is not over. Asking a suspect questions, before the known facts of a case have been verified, is... ahh... here we are."

Sajjan uncovered Dash's eyes. They were in a modern looking office meeting room. A simple round white table with four chairs. Tea had been set out.

"I have missed tea so much!" Dash announced. "Thank you."

"Help yourself. Shall we begin?"

"Yes."

"First, if you are willing, you will need to sign this acknowledgement that you accept me to defend you."

Dash signed the paper.

"You can read and write?"

"Berber, Arabic, French..." Dash didn't add that since Cleo he could understand everything he heard.

"They tell me you are a peasant, a goat... herder," Azim said, declining the ruder expression.

"They say that because I am Algerian. There are political resentments. My father was a history professor at University 1 of Algiers. He was forced out of the university because of politics and returned to our ancestral home, The Oasis."

"But you are not political?"

"As I told you."

"Well, so far, you are accused of murdering two men on a train. Tchermil, probably, by the tattoos.

"Self-defense."

"And shooting three rebel fighters at the Café Perdrix Blanc, then executing the one with the explosive vest."

"Self-defense. Public interest."

"Assaulting the attendant at the hospital?"

"I taped him to a chair. Is that still assault? I guess it's not self-defense."

"You do not seem to appreciate the trouble you are in."

"Oh, I appreciate it."

Azima stared at his yellow pad. "I have made two columns on my pad. The first is much longer, but on the plus side you also are credited with saving two wounded police officers from public execution, and providing them with emergency medical aid when you could have easily escaped."

"How many were hurt at the café?"

"Six killed, many wounded." Azima's face darkened. "If that vest had gone off, it would have been worse."

"The price of paradise," Dash grimaced. "Isn't that what they call it?"

"Nowhere is safe."

"Speaking of nowhere, where am I?"

"You are in a holding cell for uniquely dangerous individuals."

"But where?"

"On the outskirts of Rabat."

"Then you know about the attack in the Café Comedie."

"Of course."

"For your list, I got two of those guys, seeing as you are keeping score. Captain Asim of the Royal Guards got the other. Last week I was out in the desert with the Prince and he was attacked. Whether murder or kidnapping I don't know. I killed one of them in the first battle, then two more later. Captain Asim can vouch for my kills – probably the attempt on the Prince has not been made public, so you may not even know."

"That is the policy. As to your contribution, are you confessing or bragging?"

"I haven't decided, what do you think I should go with?"

"It is my job to present your case in the best possible light."

"Good. Glad to hear it."

"I'm not done listing your accomplishments, Dash Lahlou. You are also present in the Kingdom without a visa, as an Algerian national. Technically the border is closed."

"You can imagine how happy I am about that right now. I trust you have my new Algerian passport?"

The Advocate raised an eyebrow. "You can appreciate how awkward that is for my government, who wish neither criminals nor heroes."

"No, only to import a princess."

"Excuse me?" The Advocate frowned, of course not catching the reference.

"Never mind." Dash stood up and paced. "Are we fighting the rebels or are we not? Are we living as free men or as little bunnies hiding under a rock, quivering?" Dash's eyes flashed. "I've killed rebels, I may kill... others... though, to be frank, the chances of that do not look good. But tell... whomever you must tell, that I have done more to hurt the rebels in a week than your government has done in... I don't know, a year?"

"That is a political question, my young friend. Not a legal one. The prosecutor, a politically ambitious fellow, is offering an arrangement that even I, as your defender, think is generous. He will allow you to sign a document agreeing to be sent back to Algeria, and that you agree to never return. If you return, then all the original charges will be pressed against you, plus any new ones they can think up. Certainly the death penalty will be on the table."

Dash closed his eyes and allowed himself a few seconds. Home. His grandma, Addi, Baz, his friends, his dirt bike... "That makes no sense. They should be happy that I killed a few of those insects and accept my offer to kill a few more."

"You cannot be a hero, Dash Lahlou, even though you helped protect the prince, the police officers, and other brave things, because you are a foreigner.

Yet neither can you be a criminal, again because you are a foreigner, for how could the government allow such a thing? These are the ironies which enable me to still enjoy my profession."

"Officers Simo and Karim, are they okay?"

"Yes, they are recovering. They will be rewarded for your heroism."

"Your jokes are not wasted, Advocate. But truly, they were brave. They could have been jerks and got us all killed. Simo gave me his gun, and he helped shoot with his personal weapon. I am glad they will be recognized."

"They are grateful that you did not run away."

"I wanted to, but I was tired."

"That you only wounded and did not kill two of the café killers, which leaves them alive to be questioned, will not help your case."

"Why not? That makes no sense."

"You have created a conflict of jurisdiction. Should you be tried in the criminal court? Or should you be handled in the military court which deals with security matters, which, when the rebels inevitably confess, this will surely become. By leaving them alive, you have not helped yourself. The government has no obligation to put dead men on trial. They have already been judged." The advocate stared out the window. "But living men? They can always be a problem."

"I'll remember that next time," Dash groaned. "Are you an advocate for the military court also?"

"Well, the law has changed, as part of the King's reforms. Civilians can no longer be tried in military court. But... you are not a citizen... as I said, many things must still be determined.

"I see myself, in the future, with a beard almost as impressive as yours before my case is resolved."

"I don't even remember myself without this beard," Azima the Advocate mused. Were I to shave, I would probably scare myself. Are you political, Dash Lahlou? Everyone is trying to figure you out."

"I am just what the wind has blown."

The Advocate stood up to leave. "I suggest you contemplate the free ride to the train station closest to your home. Go back to your life. Whatever led you here Dash... whether chance, fate or something more profound, let it go. The Fates may push us, but we can push back."

"Whatever led me here?" Dash stared dreamily at the courtyard outside. Of course it was cobblestone. If he never saw another cobblestone in his life he would be happy.

"May I have a cigarette?"

"Certainly," Azima handed him a cheap domestic cigarette and lit it.

Dash coughed. "I don't smoke, but I am determined to learn."

"It takes only practice. So, what led you here?"

"I was sent. Probably I thought it would be an adventure. Only a man without ambition can be trusted. Is that an expression? Or did I make it up? How can I go back to what I was? It is impossible."

"Who sent you?"

"Maybe a girl's father. Maybe God. Because the girl's father could never have done what has been done. This is even stranger because I am not particularly religious, beyond what is customary."

"One begins life with a thousand questions, Dash. And ends with ten thousand, seeing as we are playing philosophers today. You have already, by the consensus of everyone who has studied your case, accomplished the impossible. But I don't think you are quite done yet – is there anything you need?"

"A blanket, cigarettes, books, a candle... am I asking for so much?"

"I will see what I can do. There is a great irony in the law," the advocate shook his head. "The greater the crime, the better the accused are treated."

"Also, I need to make a phone call."

"I will do my best."

"Thank you."

The messages are clear. "Leave Morocco", says Laila's father. "Take the government's generous offer and leave Morocco...' advises Dash's advocate. But Dash is showing some stones here and is putting the pieces together. That he sticks around has to impress Laila, right?

Chapter 46

The next day Sajjan the Jailor came and took Dash to a small room with a table, a chair, a note pad and pencil, and a phone. Dash dialed the number.

"I wish to speak with Monsieur de la Finestere, the Minister of the Interior.

"Whom may I say is calling?"

"Tell him that I, Dash Lahlou, have been arrested, and am being held in the Aljahim prison, in Rabat, in Morocco, in North Africa. They are keeping me in a well."

There was mumbling on the phone.

"No, not that I am not well, they are keeping me in a well... no, it is dry... tell monsieur that I am the one who brought his daughter, Laila out of the desert, and I was told to call if I was ever in trouble - if you ever tasted the food here, you would know."

More incomprehensible grumbling.

"L-a-h-l-o-u... Yes! That's me! I am the one who shot her in the ear." Dash put his hand over the phone and rolled his eyes. "Is no one over that?"

Click. The line went dead.

Dash lay on a thin straw mat in a clean white djerbi. The shower had been several pails of water thrown over him in another room. And it wasn't like he needed to shave. And at least his bandages had been changed. He saw Freddy's meticulous stitches on his arm for the first time. They had also, though with much muttering, given him candles, so he could re-read his Mexican wrestling magazine. He had decided to become a fan of the *lucha libre* wrestlers.

An hour later, Dash was falling asleep with the iron door clanked. Sajjan the Jailor was back, which was unusual. He handed Dash a magazine. "This just came, but I don't read English," he shrugged.

"Thank you." Dash would have been grateful for a Russian tractor catalogue. Instead it was the new issue of Teen Vogue. He didn't know there was such a thing. He thought Laila had been messing with him from the beginning.

There she was. In an emerald green silk dress, an orange scarf woven into her hair, standing in front of some petroglyphs, smiling. Maybe he had woken up in paradise after all. There was another shot of her in profile, in American blue jeans and a Dior tee shirt. The Sahara spread out behind her. This was Laila, just before getting on the doomed plane. Who else had been there, waiting to shoot them down?

Chapter 47

Dash was holding the phone so tightly it almost broke. He heard Gattopardo's voice.

"Ça vas?"

"I'm in jail in Rabat. At the bottom of a well."

"Well done."

"You're hilarious."

"Thank you. I didn't want to call until I had your bag."

"How did that go?"

"Heather was mortified about Dr. Freddy. She asked many questions about you. She's a fine looking woman."

"Oh don't tell me..." Dash groaned.

"As you know, she's on sabbatical from her restaurant," Gattopardo explained. "I was the on-shore excursion from the cruise ship – I had to win her over to get your luggage."

"I appreciate your sacrifice. Please tell Heather that I was sorry to leave so unexpectedly."

"For you, Dash, anything. I trust you've read Conrad's 'Heart of Darkness'."

"Apparently we both journeyed down the same river?"

"I had to use charm - by the way, your bag has the same weight as when you last had it."

"Thank you. I was not concerned."

"What is your situation?"

"I think they will just deport me. That's what the advocate pretty much said. Can you take whatever is necessary from my bag and get me out? Is that a possibility?

"Under the new social contract... I could do it that way. Or I could do it the old-fashioned way. It's your call, Dash, but yes, we need to get you out."

There was something in Gatto's voice that worried Dash. "Have you had any luck in Tangier?"

"I'm sorry Dash. I wanted to come and tell you in person."

"You can tell me now."

"They're gone, Dash. They were set up and robbed. They were shot. They did not suffer."

"They had bodyguards."

"Young men from the mountains are no match for *tchermil* pigs, Dash."

"Is it possible to find out who did this?"

"Perhaps."

"How soon can you get me out?"

Dash finished his call. He put down the phone and wept.

Chapter 48

Even Sajjan the Jailer became concerned when Dash refused all food. On the 3rd day, the 10th of his imprisonment, Sajjan came and sat with him. He brought a deck of cards, thinking to play, but Dash could not do it.

On the 11th day, Dash woke up to a funny but familiar smell.

"Ferrous!"

"Please forgive my perhaps inconvenient entrance," as Ferrous crouched on his hindquarters.

"How did you do this?" Dash sat up with delight. "This is a *prison!*"

"That explains the lack of… comfort." Ferrous gazed up at the high stone tower while Dash embraced him with great enthusiasm.

"Dash I came simply as a gesture of friendship. I have no power over life and death, I cannot give you more than I have given, and for that I apologize. I wish I could do more."

"But you are here, and that is enough." Dash laughed. "We try, and then we try again. Laila will absolutely kill me if she finds out I saw you and she was not here."

"Well, we don't want Laila in this situation, do we?"

"No, no. She is at the Palace, where she is treated like royalty."

"She is in grave danger, Dash. The Prince has many enemies, and she is seen as the way to manipulate him."

"Thank you for telling me."

"I came to offer you some small comfort, that you are remembered and your fate is not set."

"You give me great comfort, not small, and I only wish that Laila was here to scratch your nose."

Dash and Ferrous sat and talked for a long time and Dash was greatly comforted.

On the 11ᵗʰ day, Dash was awake and doing exercises when Sajjan the Jailer brought bread and soup. He stood inside the cell sniffing the air.

"Okay, today you get a shower, for sure."

On the 14th day of his custody, Azima the Advocate returned.

"Apparently you have friends."

"I have you. It is a blessing to see you."

"It is a blessing to be seen... the government has agreed to release you. I think it is partly as an acknowledgement of you helping to protect the Prince, for which you get no credit because officially it did not happen. But also they are trying to be more sensitive to the mood of the public."

"Which is?"

"Fear. Concern. Rebels hit a random target nearly every week, slaughtering the innocent. Punishing a man who kills rebels - when the government is hard-pressed to do so - they realize this may not play well in the medina."

"I'm glad, because I'm going to keep doing it."

"There is a car outside as we speak. I regret to lose you as a client."

"Fate, Advocate, is like our hot winds. It is hard to stand against them."

The men embraced. Sajjan the Jailor locked the iron gate behind them.

"Why do you lock it, Sajjan," Dash asked, "when there is no longer anyone inside?"

"It is closed now, this cell was only for you."

Dash carefully folded his Mexican wrestling magazine and handed it to Sajjan. "May I keep the American magazine?"

"Of course. My English has not improved since last we spoke. Perhaps if we had had more time together..."

"It would have passed pleasantly, to speak English with you."

"Thank you, Sir. All blessings to you."

It was the same silent driver as had taken Dash and Laila to Rabat, though perhaps not the same car. He was as conversant as ever. He drove Dash to a riad. He handed him an overnight bag from the trunk.

"It has been prepared for you." He jutted his chin towards the door.

Reticence, brevity. Qualities Dash aspired to. He nodded his head in approval.

Dash was humbled by the beautiful room after his time in jail. He dumped the contents of the bag on the bed. Clothes, toiletries, a fat roll of paper money tied with a rubber band. A Beretta 92 and two clips.

Dash bathed and ate a few almonds. He dressed and went out to an internet café and searched the news for stories about the murder of his parents. Other jewelry dealers and pharmacies had been hit. The rebels were desperate to finance their operations, and were not above using street punks to do it.

The police were investigating. There were no arrests, and no bodies. The police presumed they had been dumped in the ocean, which was customary. Dash had to face that he would never see his parents again. And his grandma had to grieve her son. His place was there, to comfort her. Again he had failed.

He searched Laila online. Each engagement festivity was each more splendid than the one before. These stories were full of images of her with children and the elderly, at a hospital or in some village. She looked happy.

The stories did not show the images of the villages burning, the bodies of the men lined up in rows.

He had once read about quicksand in some American boys' adventure book. The more you struggled the more quickly you sank. That's how he felt right now.

He stood on the sidewalk outside the internet café. Busy people spilled around him like he was a rock in a stream. He walked back to the hotel. As usual he took a pillow and blanket and slept on the floor.

In the morning Gatto picked him up. The driver was the same. They drove to an industrial area by the docks. Huge freighters strained at their ropes. Dash had never seen such things and his eyes bulged.

"Where do they go?"

"Wherever there is deep water," Gattopardo said. "As a boy, I read 'Two Years Before the Mast', 'Moby Dick' and many other adventure books as I dreamed of going to sea. What did you dream of, Dash?"

"To go to school, and become a doctor. But I fear my father was too political."

"The harsh winds of politics don't have beautiful names like scirroco or ghibli, yet they burn just the same... here we are."

Dash nodded.

"I'm sorry, Dash, but you have to know, so you can grieve and be done with it."

What had been a warehouse was now a crime scene. There were scrubbed and only faded blood stains on the floors and walls. Bullet holes in the walls. A robbery gone bad. Probably on purpose. How innocent his parents had been. He said a quiet prayer. Gatto sat on a wooden crate smoking Gitanes, careful not to drop ash on his expensive suit.

"What can I do for you, my young friend?"

"Can we learn who did this?" Dash choked on the words.

"Probably a local rival of mine called The Turk. He controls the ports, export of refugees, illegal documents. His front business is import/export. Uses local punks for muscle. One of his side businesses is to drop bodies far out at sea where they will never be found. This probably wasn't supposed to be murder, he is not known for that, but that is what happens when you use cheap, stupid help."

"Where can I find him?"

"A casino in Marrakech this weekend. Partying. I made a plan."

"I don't want to get arrested again. I won't get lucky twice."

"I have arranged a job for you, as a bellboy. Work a few days, learn the layout of the hotel. You take a cart of empty luggage to his room. The gun will be in the outside pocket of the smallest piece of luggage. There will be a car waiting for you afterwards."

"Is it inevitable that each death leads to the next?"

"Oh yes. The path narrows."

Chapter 49

Gatto had given him I.D. papers and taken custody of his bag and personal effects. He would be provided with a clean gun. The usual driver took him to Marrakech.

The Bell Captain appreciated his language skills. Several uneventful days shuffling bags around for mostly nice people on vacation. At first the elevator had terrified him, but the thought of stairs was worse. Dash was astonished at how rich people spent their time, laying by the pool, eating in restaurants, gambling. Several of the European women smiled and asked for his company in the afternoons, while their husbands gambled, but he was in no mood. He would just smile and say he had to work.

Finally the room number came by text. With one photo of The Turk. He immediately deleted it. He picked up the luggage from the storage room and rolled the cart into the elevator. He had already figured out how to stop the elevator between floors. He did that now and quickly looked for the gun. Nothing. Again Dash frantically searched the luggage. Found it.

The man who answered the door was chubby and pale for a Turk, probably naked under the bathrobe. Dash didn't like the way he looked at him, but he matched the photo of The Turk he had been shown.

"You can leave that," The Turk gestured at the luggage with his chin.

Dash's eyes searched the room. There was another door, closed.

"I'm having some trouble with the shower," The Turk continued. "Could you take a look?" he said, flashing a 100 d note under Dash's eyes.

"Do you want it hot—or cold?" Dash smiled flirtatiously, seeing his chance.

"I want it anyway I can get it," The Turk smiled, showing interest. "You're a beautiful boy, if you don't mind my saying."

"I don't mind at all. What are you going to do about it?"

Dash turned and walked into the shower, putting the water on medium heat. "Is this okay?" Dash called out. The man came into the shower, already naked.

"Get undressed," he purred. "We can shower together."

The shower head had a long hose. As The Turk stepped forward to check the water Dash stepped back as if to undress but instead rabbit-punched the man in the kidney. All the breath came out of him. Dash took out the gun. The man curled into the corner of the shower, his hands extended, as if they were protection.

Dash put away the gun, his eyes full of darkness. Instead he wrapped the shower hose tightly around his neck and began to strangle him, then stopped. The Turk slumped to the floor. Dash turned off the water and sat on a plastic stool. He stared at the man coldly.

The Turk again twisted his body into the furthest corner of the shower, his back against the wall, choking, rubbing his neck.

"What do you want?" He gasped.

"I have questions."

The Turk nodded.

"I want to know about a robbery in Tangier, not more than two months ago. One or several thugs murdered my parents in Tangier, while stealing assorted, uncut jewels. In fact, you probably don't even know that they kept the jewels from you, thinking they were clever – which is why you are alive. I don't think you ordered the murder, or your mouth would be full of dirt."

"Murder is stupid." The Turk nodded with interest.

"Perhaps. But I have a problem. Killing you does not punish them, and I do not know who they are."

"I have four armed men in the other room. They are experienced. I think you have a larger problem."

Dash shrugged. "They will die for no reason, because you will already be dead."

The Turk's eyes believed Dash. "What do you want?"

"I want you to investigate the robbery, and the killings."

"Yes. I want to know who ran a stupid side hustle without telling me, because the police also will consider me an easy target for blame. We are on the same page."

"Send a message through Gattopardo. And you owe him a favor. He counseled against just killing you."

"We are both older now." The Turk kept rubbing his neck. "I understand. Do you work for him?"

"I'm a student. But he has been a friend. Are we in agreement?"

"Yes. You have my word. Do you want them dead?"

"I don't know. I just hurt. To my profound disappointment, I am learning that death changes nothing about your pain."

Dash went back into the living room and stripped off his wet uniform and clothes and left them on the floor. He dressed in a hotel logo'd robe and flip flops from the closet and wrapped a towel around his neck. He unplugged a clock radio. He cut the cord with his pocket knife and stripped the wires down to the copper and tied them together in a knot and grabbed the T.V. remote.

He went into the living room portion of the suite. Four thugs playing cards. They stared at him.

"Your boss needs some assistance."

The men stared at his gun and his fake bomb. Dash made them strip off their clothes and crowded them all into the shower area with The Turk. Then he locked the bathroom door.

"I've set this for ten minutes delay." Dash yelled through the door trying not to laugh, he was suddenly enjoying this. "You have nine minutes and fifty nine seconds to disassemble it."

He took the emergency stairs down, in case of cameras in the elevator. He walked into the Bell Boys change room and got his own clothes out of the small locker. Luckily there was no one else there.

The car was there as promised. He dialed Gattopardo.

"Thank you for the car and the weapon and the job, it was fascinating, but I did not complete the task."

"There was no completion, only a choice. It was yours to make."

"I traded his life for information. I hope he will contact you with it."

"And he agreed?"

"He didn't have a choice."

"Yes... do you still feel anger?"

"I just feel pain."

"The pain will last, I am sorry. But come back right away. We have, sadly, a new problem."

"What?" Dash frowned.

"The Prince Facile, Abbas, called me, personally. Tell the driver to hurry."

Ferrous the mumbling prophet with the ripe bouquet. Yes Laila is in deep peril and Dash is going to have to swallow his pain and rescue her, if he can. Or is she weary of danger and vulnerable? Who could blame her? Ready to give in to the Prince and drown in five star luxury? Which was it going to be? I stared at Laila and readied my pencil.

Chapter 50

Dash sat on a couch in Gatto's office, his fingers steepled and his face stormy.

"I will call the Prince back."

"Yes, I'm ready."

"I'll put him on speaker," Gatto said as he made the call. Finally they were on the line.

"Prince Facile, I have Dash Lahlou with me now."

"Listen, Dash, my friend. I'm sorry. I have no right to call upon you, I know."

"What's going on?"

"They have taken Laila."

"Who?"

"Laila de la Finestere."

"No, who took her?"

"Rebels."

"I see her on TV, on the internet. She is always surrounded by soldiers. How is this possible?"

"I don't like to think there are traitors in our army, guys, but sometimes they take a soldier's family, to get information. They stop at nothing. We doubled security after the attack on me and still they grabbed her. I am beside myself."

"What are you doing about it?"

"Recalling Asim. Putting a team together. Calling you. Are you in?"

"Assassins tried to kill me on a train, to recover the gold you gave me. If you wanted it back, you could have just asked me."

"Why would I kill you? I owe you."

"Thank you for saying that, I believe you. But who else knew my plans? Your plans?"

"We can look into that, Dash, there are many people involved in organizing my life and maybe there are some I cannot trust. But for now I have to get Laila back, you can name your price."

"You have a hole in your security. We were betrayed at the Café Comedie. You can ask Laila – the guy knew she was there. She told me there was no doubt in his eyes. And you were betrayed at our games outing, which cost the lives of good young men in the Royal Guard. And now Laila? I would sleep with a gun under your pillow, your Highness, if I were you. It's not my place to say, I am sorry, but there is only so much luck in the world."

Gatto put his hand over his eyes and grimaced. "We have to get Laila back, and you know you can't make a deal with these rebels, your Highness. You know they are only good for death."

"Why do you think I called? Dash, you've killed more rebels than anyone. Your legend grows. You are also the only one besides Laila who has seen the caves and lived. I am asking you to brief my team, just that would be a big help."

"I agree. Please make the arrangements," Dash said to Gatto as he stood up and left the room. Gatto took the phone off speaker and leaned back in his chair to finish the call.

Dash went and sat at a table outside the café. The sun was warm on his face.

"The Prince could have left you to rot in that round-walled prison. Or he could arrest you now. He is not the problem."

Dash nodded. "I know."

Gatto sipped his espresso. "So clear your head. We will go together. I will take half a dozen of my most reliable men and we will coordinate with Asim and the Royal Guards. We leave for the staging area in the morning."

Chapter 51

The Prince declined to sit so no one did. Dash and Asim had already briefed the Royal Guard in this training auditorium and they had gone off to gear up. That left Dash, Gattopardo, Captain Asim, Laila's father, the Prince and various of his assistants.

"Who is this?" Finestere gestured unpleasantly at Gattopardo who had shown up in a vintage army jacket, American jeans and his usual white Gucci loafers.

"One of my advisors," Captain Asim said pleasantly enough. "What is your concern, Monsieur de la Finestere? We are on the clock here."

"We are risking young lives," Finestere gestured to the empty seats where the soldiers had been, "when we have an agreement in place to simply pay the ransom. I myself am willing to take the risk to deliver the ransom to the rebels in exchange for Laila. The Kingdom will not be out of pocket as I will include the amount in the marriage gift, and as you know, the investment contemplated in the destroyed Algerian and Moroccan villages which have been attacked is generous."

"We have a standing policy," the Prince began, "to not pay ransom, and I have confidence in our soldiers. That said, Monsieur de la Finestere, if we can speak frankly within these walls, you and I both far too invested in this matter to give the best counsel. It is already haunting me that Laila is in peril and that I cannot participate in the actual rescue, aside from the risk to our men. Of course I personally prefer to pay. But I suggest that we defer to Captain Asim in this matter."

"Captain Asim, with all due respect, is a hammer. A hammer sees everything as a nail. I suggest a more nuanced approach is needed. "

"Captain Asim, please walk us through this – again?"

"All ransom buys is more kidnappings and more ransoms. I referenced Italy's experience in the 1970's in the briefing. We have good intel that the rebels have consolidated at their volcano on the coast. Very likely that is where Laila is. We have good information from Dash here about how the rebels are organized and about the interior of the volcano. While they may individually be good fighters and dangerous, they are not trained or equipped anywhere near the level of the Royal Guards. We have a unique opportunity to profoundly decimate their strength."

"You advise a full scale military operation with Laila in the middle of it?! Let me recover Laila, then you can follow up with your operation before they can disperse. You can blow the mountain into sand for all I care. Secondly, Captain, the track record of the regular military – not your Royal Guards - against the southern rebels is not, so far, successful. The Kingdom is hit nearly every week, terrifying the population. I think young Dash Lahlou here has more 'kills' than any of those units."

"It's not just about Laila, Monsieur de la Finistere," Dash surprised himself with the sound of his own voice. All eyes were upon him and he could see that Finistere was pissed that he had spoken up. "If it were, your strategy would be correct. But from what Laila and I witnessed both in villages and at The Holy Mountain, and from what we know from reports from other villages, their mountain contains hundreds of slaves. Women, children and old men. Your ransom doesn't buy one of them, and 'blowing them to sand' from the air or from the water, doesn't save one of them. Your daughter Laila's first concern in our journey was never for herself, her own safety. From the first village she wanted to go after the stolen children, and with God's blessing we were able to send about twenty or so women and children back to my village. She never thought of herself, and if you walk in there today and said, 'Okay, Laila, let's go', you are free, she will say to you 'what about the others'. That is Laila, that is who she is."

"Captain Asim?" The Prince gestured.

"Let's go."

Chapter 52

Nothing had worked. Attacking a mountain is never an easy thing.

Dash and Laila were on their knees, hands tied behind their backs. They were on top of the volcano, which was groaning and shaking and leaking lava, on a broad stone balcony that gave a view of the desert to the east.

The Jinn paced behind them. The Jinn stood taller than any of his fighters. He was handsome, as demons go, though his skin had a strange blue glow and tiny scorpions climbed upon his body. His eyes were not eyes, but smokeless flame. All Dash could do was stare.

Below them the battle raged between Royal Guards and the rebel forces.

The Jinn looked at Dash. "So you are the one who protected her and brought her to me..." the Jinn said in a congenial tone. "I offer you a place at my side. I have an army now, all I need is a bride," He glared at Laila, who stared at the rocks below. "Look, Laila, I can offer you all this!" He gestured his arms wide.

They stared out at the landscape of scrub and rocks and dust, with the sand of the Sahara beyond it. It didn't matter. He had found Laila. The earth shook and an explosion above rained rocks down on them.

"Take them to my cave, to contemplate my offer," the Jinn said to one of his officers. "Remind them that time is short, that I will take care of this enemy and then it will be decided who joins in the victory."

The long stone hallway was not one Dash knew, neither did he recognize the side tunnels, there were so many. It was empty. The tunnels were much hotter than on his previous visit. Then there was a loud crack behind them and Dash turned to see a Royal Guard lower his weapon. The rebel officer lay on the ground, quite dead.

"Thank you!" Dash exclaimed. "Cut us free."

"Dash? It's me, Sami."

They embraced awkwardly. "This is Laila, maybe you know each other?"

Sami saluted her.

Dash frowned, "Should I be doing that?"

"That's a great idea, Dash!" Laila laughed. "And Sami, thank you for rescuing us."

Sami cut them free, and Dash stripped the armor from the dead man.

"Arms up," and Dash slid it on to Laila and adjusted it. Then he handed Laila the assault rife, taking the side arm for himself.

"We need to go," Sami said.

"Do you know how to get out?" Dash asked.

"No, I got separated from my team."

"We just have to stick together. I'll take point, I know this place a little."

"Yes, I was in your briefing."

"My lousy inadequate briefing. How is the battle going?"

"It is fierce. I hope we get re-enforcements and air support."

Dash started a light jog through the tunnels, trying to find something familiar, or smell fresh air. Then they were thrown to the ground by another earthquake.

"This whole place is going to blow," Sami announced.

"Keep moving – listen for water. There is a giant waterfall which will take us out to the ocean. They don't guard it."

Dash helped Laila to her feet and they were on the move again. There was no apparent exit, the rumbling sounds and distant chaos were not directional at all, though they seemed to be headed down. Then there was a four way stop to the right there were marks on the wall that looked familiar. They went right until Dash recognized a dug-out rock face he had worked on. A thin line of lava was running urgently across the floor.

"I know where we are. Let's get out of here." A few more tunnels and Dash heard the waterfall. They shouldered their weapons and jumped in the running water. Then they burst out into fresh air, bent-over, panting, and climbed up on the rocky part of the beach. On their left was the ocean, and the small port with the fishing boats tied to the pier. On their right they could hear the fighting.

Laila dropped to one knee and scanned the rocks above them. "Sniper."

"I'll stand up," Dash said, "You guys spot him."

"Crack!" Stone fragments pierced Dash's cheek and he dropped to the ground.

"Crack, crack." Laila and Sami both fired and a body thumped on the rocks above. "Let's take the beach down to the Command tent, then I can find my unit."

"Let's go then. Take point, Sami, on your shoulder."

They jogged lightly along the beach, away from the main battle. There was a lot of debris, from kelp to tree trunks.

Laila slowed down to match Dash's pace. "You used to be faster."

"Then I met you," Dash grinned.

"If we get out of here... Dash, I'm done. I want to go away with you, anywhere. I don't want to be a princess or a Queen or a Teen Vogue model. I want to lay in the sand and look at the stars and hold your ha..." blood splashed from under Laila's arm, the one spot that was not protected by the body armor. She stumbled and fell to her knees. Dash looked ahead and saw the shooter, laying behind a water-logged tree trunk. He raised his gun but Sami was faster.

Crack. Crack.

Dash saw the man's head explode from Sami's hit. Then Dash saw the second man throw down his weapon and run away from them. He aimed for the center of the man's back and squeezed.

Crack.

He shouldered his rifle and picked up Laila in his arms.

Sami pulled a large gauze pad out his gear and showed Dash how to press it against the wound under her arm. Laila groaned in pain.

"Dash, I'll lead you to the Med tent, let's go!"

They ran. Then they were off the beach and into the scrub towards the tents. They felt yet another earthquake under their feet and a commotion behind them but there was no time to look back.

Fireballs of lava exploded like little meteors around them. Dash stumbled in a straight line, there was no point in trying to dodge them. All he could do was stare at Sami's back. Behind them the volcano was starting to bleed into the sea and the column of steam and smoke rose high in the sky.

"Almost there," Dash gasped to Laila.

"I'm so sorry Dash."

"Don't talk."

They reached the field hospital. Medics took her from his arms, Sami and Dash fell to their knees in the sand. Ashes fell around them like snowflakes. Someone handed them canteens.

"Salud," Dash banged his canteen against Sami's. "We could not have escaped without you."

"My job, man. I have to go find my unit."

Dash took out his phone and took Sami's picture. "Laila and I will want to thank you, after."

They fell to the ground from new explosions. Dash sat up, catching his breath, getting oriented as Sami pointed. "Look, those are our new Navy Panther helicopters! Now we can kick some ass!"

Dash could see them banking back out to sea after their missiles exploded on the volcano.

"Thank you!"

Sami and Dash clasped hands and then Sami was gone.

An orderly ran up to him. "You're Dash, right? The doctor, he needs you."

Dash stood up, nodding as he glugged water and ran to the medical tents.

A blood splattered field doctor looked up from working on a soldier. "You Dash? She keeps asking for you. Before I knocked her out. Medical chopper's coming. But she needs blood right now - and we're out."

"Do you know who she is?"

"Doesn't matter if she's the Queen of Siam, buddy. She'll die just like the rest of us if I have no blood to give her. What type are you?"

"Red? I have no idea. I am not a soldier. Take as much as you need. For the others, too. I don't care."

"Okay." The doctor managed a grimace where a smile might have once been.

"In the next tent. Lay on the cot beside her and they will hook you up. The nurse will check your blood type.

Dash could hardly move the tent flap. Someone helped him onto the cot. He heard the hum of a generator. He saw a thumbs up from the nurse. Every other cot was full of wounded.

"Take as much as you need."

He looked across at Laila who smiled weakly.

"You came."

"Of course."

"Did you...?"

"Yes."

"Helicopter is coming... they told me... Dash, I don't want to go back to the palace, I want to stay with you."

"That's just the morphine talking. But right now I'm going to give you blood. Doctor says you lost a lot and you need it. We can talk later."

"But they're taking me... I want you to... what? Dash... your blood? They can't use your blood! It's impossible."

"There is no one else. Gatto is with the soldiers fighting. Everyone is fighting."

Dash could see tears running from Laila's eyes. She nodded. He lay down beside her on the next cot and the nurse hooked them up. He reached across and they held hands as his blood flowed into her through the plastic tubes. "I saw your magazine, Laila. You are so beautiful."

"So next time I tell you something will you believe me?"

"Yes," Dash whispered as leaned over and he kissed her.

An hour later Dash stood under the Sahara sunset as the medical helicopter taking Laila back to the hospital rose into the burning sky. A hand offered a French cigarette. A lighter flared. It was Gatto, in a blood spattered camo jacket and white Gucci loafers, an assault rifle on his shoulder. Dash took the cigarette. He was grateful.

"You didn't go with her?" Gatto's eyes flickered in the light.

"I'm not wounded. Are you okay?"

"Sure. Just mopping up now. They are looking for Saif's body."

"Oh yes, the Sword of Faith. They won't find it. He is gone with the Jinn. Did you see that thing?"

"The stories were true. A demon inside a volcano. An army of scorpions..." Gatto shook his head.

I am worried for Captain Asim. Have you seen him? I would think some of those caves will be booby-trapped."

"Captain Asim knows what he is doing. The volcano might just melt down everything."

"You didn't have to come."

"What and miss the fun? You haven't lived until you've emptied a clip into a mutant scorpion - and while we are on the subject, you know I apologize."

"For what?"

"For thinking your scorpion story was a little... embellished."

"Embellished? Really? You saw my back!"

"Just a little...what will we do for excitement when this is over, Dash?"

"Do I have any gold left?"

"You have all of it left."

"You didn't pay the Azim the Advocate?" Dash frowned.

"He wouldn't take it. You have an unusual effect on people, Dash. You make them want to be better than they are."

"You can't be serious."

"Even me," Gatto smiled. "I could have sold Laila for a fortune, but I have to look at this face each morning. Maybe I want to be invited to fancy parties at the palace...sorry...my point is that I like my life exactly as it is. Do you feel the same since giving Laila blood, or different?"

"Weaker, tired. But maybe that is, how do you call... the battle fatigue? Anyway, I did not give her all of it. How much do they take? A litre? I will need some of your wine, to replenish. Do you make a red, or is the pink okay?"

"Laila will be even more amazing now, you have shared blood, you are joined in ways I can't explain - can I show you something?"

"Sure," Dash pinched out the butt of his cigarette and put it in his pocket. He didn't want to spoil the sand.

"Hold my jacket. And my weapon..."

Dash took them and watched as Gatto pulled off his bloodied tee shirt. His eyes widened as he saw the old scars, vertical lines in the shape of a bear's paw.

"You have met... Ferrous?"

"Of course. How many freaking spirit animals do you think there are in the mountains?" Gatto chuckled.

"When?"

"It must be thirty years. I was a young man, like you." Gatto stared at the look on Dash's face with delight. How long he had waited for this moment. "He told me to wait, to wait as long as was necessary for a young man with the same mark and then to help him in any way I could. During that time I would be protected and prosper in the human world."

"How did you know? You must have known many young men."

"Yes, and I always had someone check them for markings. But with you I just knew. And I knew Laila was the one, the one who was promised. There was never doubt. With you? Yeah, doubt. Lots of doubt."

They laughed together.

"What about Cleo? The snake? Were you ever bitten?"

"No, that is on a whole other level that you have now passed on to Laila through your blood. I was given strength, stamina, the ability to read people... your job was to protect Laila and help fulfill her destiny."

"Laila doesn't want her destiny, Gatto. She doesn't want it. What can she do?"

"Neither do you, but here we are... by the way, you never asked me about my name."

"Gatto?"

"It means 'leopard' in Italian. Ferrous was messing with you. Bears have a weird sense of humor."

"Ferrous visited me, in the round prison."

"You're kidding?"

"No, I thought I was delirious until the next day the Jailor came in and could smell that he'd been there."

"Did he tell you what is Laila's destiny?"

"Laila is prophesied to rule as Queen, unite the people, and be much loved."

Dash could not have said it with less enthusiasm, and Gattopardo watched his eyes.

Dash slumped in the sand, shaking his head. "She can really do such things?"

"Because of the blood you gave her. You closed the circle."

Gattopardo sat beside Dash on the sand, smoking and watching as Royal Guards helped the rescued women and children onto trucks which would take them to the nearest civilian hospital a few hours up the coast.

"What will happen now?"

"The rebels are retreating south. Remember that Asim warned us in the briefing that we cannot chase them without the U.N. raising a stink and creating an international incident. They will disappear into the refugee camps and re-organize. They are trapped by the sand wall and cannot go inland across the desert."

"And it will be Laila who will calm the waters at home?"

"It's the Sahara desert. There are no waters to calm," Gatto laughed and Dash blushed.

"Seriously, it will be Laila who will speak," Gatto began, "in the government and to the media, to convince the Moroccan and Algerian governments to fund the refugees and slaves return to the burnt villages, and to improve the standards of life in Tindour and other camps." Gatto lit another cigarette. "It will be Laila who visits the villages and brings supplies and teachers and stations soldiers there to protect them in the future. The soldiers will be chosen from young men who can become married with the young widows and become fathers to the broken children. That is what you have done, Dash. You and Laila."

"And what do I do now?" Dash's voice ached. "I want to return to who I was. But I can never be that boy again, nor can I be what I have become."

"Shall we join up with Asim, and hunt rebels in the mountains? I felt twenty years younger in the fight, but I suspect that feeling doesn't last."

Dash laughed.

"Or..." Gatto looked away. "We could leave for The Oasis tomorrow. To honor your parents and arrange a pension for your grandmother. And ask the elders for their blessing that I take care of you, so that you can go to school and become your heart's desire, and I can fulfill my own promise to Ferrous."

"My heart's desire? You're awfully poetic for a scoundrel and a thief."

"Perhaps poetry is all we have left."

"Give me another cigarette, please." Dash paused. "It's true, already I grow weary of death. Not one death has returned to me what I have lost. Anyway, what chance do we have against our fate?"

"I propose that we find our friend Asim," Gattopardo stood and brushed off the sand. "It worries me still that we don't know who betrayed the Café Comedie rendezvous."

"The traitor is Laila's father."

Gatto was stunned. "How is this so?"

"It was his brother's failed plan. A fake kidnapping, collect ransom from the Prince's family – you have taught me many things. Also, how strongly he offered to deliver the ransom in cash to the rebels."

"So he sent thugs to rob and kill you on the train, to get the royal gold back?"

"Yes, I told him my travel plan, but then I changed my mind. He still found me. I don't know how."

"Are you going to tell Laila, or is this going to be the first secret between you?" Gatto smirked the smirk of experience and Dash made a sour face as they walked towards the volcano.

"You could tell her, Gatto," Dash tried to laugh. "Even I believe in her fate. But she doesn't want to be Queen. Can we disappear? "How do we defy a fate that seems to be carved out of stone? I met a demon today, by the way."

"How did that go?"

"He offered me a job. But he wants Laila as his bride, so I declined."

"Do you blame him?" Gatto laughed.

Dash smiled. "Gatto, I have a plan. Will you help us?"

"I promised Ferrous. Of course I will help you."

Chapter 53

Laila was two weeks in the hospital. Dash stayed at the riad by one of Gatto's cafés and visited her each day. Then he read for hours at the Mohammed V medical library and imagined himself becoming a student there.

Dash always brought flowers and sat at Laila's bedside. Armed guards were outside the door.

"I'm almost better, they re-inflated my lung and it is working perfectly."

"Good, you can join me on my next adventure."

"France, Dash. We can disappear into the South of France. I have been there with my father. You would love it."

"It takes a year in France just to study for the medical school entrance exams, before you even get in, and they only let in maybe 10%. Let me talk to Gatto."

"I hear hesitation."

"I like Abbas. I don't want to betray him."

"I will talk to him. It is an arranged marriage, I mean I am fond of him, but..."

"'Fond' is the kiss of death for a guy, right?" Dash grinned.

"Yes, well, you should be happy that I was never fond of you, Dash, it was either love or hate," Laila laughed.

A nurse rang the bell. It was time. Dash gave Laila a kiss. "Tomorrow."

"Tomorrow."

Chapter 54

Dash and Laila went to the address Gatto had provided. Dash did not take a gun. It was a warehouse in the docks where The Turk kept an office. There was heavy security, but they were expected.

They were given comfortable chairs and tea. Today The Turk was wearing a tan linen suit, white shirt and a thin black knitted tie. His shaved head was shiny in the harsh industrial light.

"Most of my crimes are not violent," The Turk sighed, as he punctuated his remarks with a fly swatter. "I don't put up much of a front," he said as he wacked the fly. "What I *am* good at is import/export, smuggling via shipping containers – not people - and also documents. I love fake documents. I don't have much over-lap with Gatto. I take pride in my documents. You did me a great service in demonstrating the deficiencies of my security, Dash, for which I am responsible, and I am happy to help you without charge," The Turk giggled. "The thing with the bomb clock radio?" He looked at Laila. "Did he tell you about that one? Genius. I would tip my hat to you, if I had one."

The Turk spoke without irony, Laila raised an eyebrow while Dash took a deep breath. "We will need two French passports, in fact we will need two entirely new identities."

"May I see your current passports?"

They handed them over. Laila's was reviewed without comment. But he looked at Dash's very closely.

"You are Algerian, also?"

"Yes."

"Do you work for Algerian intelligence?"

"No," Dash frowned.

"Do you know that this passport, which looks quite new, has a tracker imbedded in it? The Algerian intelligence service will know where you are every minute of the day – this is like the old school DRS style. I thought they were all purged."

"My father is the Minister of the Interior of Algeria," Laila interjected. "It is a difficult time with the change of government."

"Then your father has a lot of friends from the old days, Miss."

"They would know where I am, that I am here, now?" Dash continued.

"Well, technically they will always know where this passport is. Not quite as good as a sub-cutaneous one, but if the carrier always has it on him... of course some people stick their passport in a drawer and never think of it until vacation... but that is not you, is it?"

"No."

"Miss Laila, your father would have the connections to get you a good French passport, you don't have to come on the black market for such a thing..."

"He doesn't know."

"Young love creates courage. I admire you."

"It's much worse than that," Laila smiled.

"Well the first thing is to get your pictures, which we can do now, then I need a few days to build your new pasts, your identities. Are you going to be married? It's not mandatory, but it helps if I know such things..."

"We're..."

"...Just kids..."

"...we have to go to..."

"...university..."

"As I said, it is not mandatory."

"My father tried to kill him," Laila said abruptly, gesturing to Dash. "That's why he was so quick to get Dash this new passport. "And my father is not one to give up on his obsessions."

"Then we must make a good photograph, in case it is the last. But for now Miss Laila, my assistant will take you for your photo."

"Sure, sure, may I touch up my make-up?"

When Laila had gone The Turk pulled open a drawer and took out a carved wooden box and opened it in front of Dash. Jewels. Emeralds, diamonds and sapphires. Large and uncut but very beautiful. Dash just stared.

"I did their passports, Dash. I gave them new identities. I faked the murder. Your parents are not dead, at least they weren't when they left here. And I bought these stones from them. They had plenty of cash to make a new start in Europe, these stones are excellent."

"Where?"

"I cannot tell you out of professional discretion. I'm sorry. Many clients move on beyond what we set up for them. You'd be surprised how many people want to disappear, Dash. I know that doesn't make you feel any better. Maybe your parents had enemies from your father's politics and they wanted to protect you by leaving. Can you try and think of it that way?"

"I can't think of it any way, honestly. I feel like my head just exploded, between my story and Laila's."

"Let's take your picture... wait... your passport is extraordinarily rare, I've never seen one, it could be valuable to me. If you let me keep it, you can choose a stone for your lady, perhaps this?" The Turk picked up a large cloudy emerald. "Properly cut, it will match her eyes. You can get it done well in France. Set it in pink gold – something simple."

"That's a great idea," Dash stood up as Laila came back in the room. She saw the look on Dash's face.

The Turk knew the blows that had been received. "Let's shoot Dash, then I will call Gatto to come and pick you up. And I promise to make peace with him. I will telephone you Dash, in a few days. Do we have a deal?"

"Yes... Laila, are we going forward?"

"Yes. To the stars."

Chapter 55

Gatto saw how sad both Dash and Laila were, so he took them to his favorite seafood restaurant on the Atlantic side, where they sat out on the broad terrace, drank icy Champagne and relaxed watching the waves.

"They say you can't get a true bouillabaisse any more because there are no *rascasse* left in the Mediterranean, Gatto explained. But that's not true, you just have to have friends among the real fishermen, who keep the good stuff for themselves and their families."

"Best meal of my life," Laila was finally smiling.

"Don't worry Laila, enjoy," Dash grinned. "Gatto will not speak of anything profound until we are finished and have moved on to the desert, the petit café – and the digestif."

"I am not worried, Dash, Gatto and I have our own relationship going. Remember, I met him before you did."

"Sure, in the trunk of a car."

"I'll drink to that glorious day," Gatto raised his glass and they toasted.

"Dash how do you feel about spending a few days with Heather Burrows, the American chef? Do you remember that she rescued you in your hour of need?"

"Oh really Dash?" Laila was taking interest. "Another story I haven't heard? What needs are we talking about...?"

"Umm... why?" Dash blushed, his voice squeaking a little.

"I've invited her to go sailing with us, a little vacation to Cannes and Nice... on a charter sailboat – two cabins. We'll sail across the Mediterranean, get you settled with papers and banking and your new identities, enjoy the café life, then Heather and I sail back. You stay in France and begin your new life."

"This is getting real, isn't it?" Laila squeezed Dash's hand under the table.

"As soon as your papers are ready. Heather will arrive tomorrow, and I have found the boat I like."

Gatto's phone buzzed. "Excuse me," he said, then looked at the text.

He leaned forward. "Dash, The Turk says your passport with the tracker is on a courier flight to New York City – and several forwarding addresses after that, culminating, I believe, in Anchorage, Alaska. Laila, that will keep your father busy for a little while."

"I thought The Turk could sell it for a lot of money?" Dash asked.

"Eventually, but for now it will circle the world. It is his gesture to you, an apology for his role in your pain..." Gatto lifted the Champagne bottle to top up Laila's glass.

"Well," Dash reached into his pocket and took out a tiny cloth bag. He turned to Laila. "I was going to do this in France, but why not now?"

He rolled the large emerald out onto Laila's hand. She gasped.

"It's so... beautiful!"

"It's an emerald. From my family. We can get it cut and set for a ring in Nice, I am sure. That's what The Turk said, anyway."

"Or in my situation, a terrific earring!"

"You're not going to let that go, are you?" Dash groaned.

"And why would I? It's so much fun... wait... I smell something," Laila scrunched up her nose.

Ferrous the Bear had climbed up onto the terrace from the beach, he was soaking wet and salty and covered with kelp. He crouched beside their table and yawned. They looked around but no one else was reacting.

"I am happy to see you all together, my friends. Gatto, you are older."

"Yes... I am pleased, considering the alternative, and to see you also."

"Laila, you blossom like a flower. May I get a selfie with you? No one in the forest believes how lovely you are. They accuse me of... exaggeration. Can you believe that?"

"It would be my honor, Ferrous. Are you well? We speak of you often."

"Oh, I am the same. Grumpy, but today is suddenly better. Dash, your station in life has much improved since our last meeting. Can you order me some sushi?"

"Sure, Ferrous, sure. Sit and relax, we've got all night."

Gatto looked over his shoulder for the waiter. "Monsieur, more Champagne!"

The End. Maybe.

Epilogue

In the fullness of time, Gatto legally adopted Dash Lahlou. They moved to the South of France, buying a villa and vineyards above the port town of Frejus, known for its Roman ruins and many antiquities. It has a beautiful view of the Mediterranean. When things calmed down, Heather the American chef sold her American restaurant. She and Gatto were married. Ferrous the Bear came to the ceremony—after bathing—and ate all the smoked salmon.

Dash's grandmother managed the staff of the house, shared her cooking secrets with Heather and fussed over all of them. Heather published numerous cook books and ran a popular cooking blog from the villa. Gatto opened a new café in the town, and again sold his own wine there.

Dash cleaned his weapon for the last time and locked it in a drawer.

Dash and Laila studied diligently and in time became doctors and worked for Médicins Sans Frontieres, which delivers doctors and supplies to the worst sites of war and catastrophy in the world.

Neither Gattopardo nor Dash nor Laila were invited to parties at the palaces large or small. Though sometimes Asim, who was now a general, would visit and stay with them. They would talk long into the night and drink very good wine.

After Laila had their first child, her private enthusiasm became to learn all the constellations which could be seen from the house. She learned how they moved with the seasons. She acquired a telescope, so as to see clearly Orion, Big Bear and Little Bear, so that she could remember to tell their child about their love in the Atlas Mountains, like in a story book.

The End. Mostly.

The clock decided to work again. It ticked 4 p.m. and I put down my pencils and stretched. I just finished drawing Laila's beautiful emerald ring after it had been cut and mounted. I stretched. My back needs to be amputated – preferably as soon as possible. I loaded my back-pack except for my fat notebook. I stretched my fingers.

"Okay kids," Mr. Mulch closed his book with a dusty thump. "I will be very happy to see none of you next Saturday. School resumes Monday at 8:00 a.m. Show up."

I stood up. Laila was putting on her stilettos. I waited patiently in front of her, luckily the fake Swede had bolted. Anyway Dash had killed him. I don't hold a grudge.

"Hey Dash," Laila stood up. "What have you been working on so diligently?"

"Oh... I draw a little... and I wrote a story, and I kind of put you in it," I stared at the floor, the words just tumbled out. "I needed a feisty girl who would inspire people."

Then I just put my notebook on her desk and stood there like an idiot. Laila picked it up and flipped through the pages.

"These drawings are amazing...well this is something that might get a girl's attention – may I read it?

"Sure."

"Are you in the story too?"

That was when I really blushed and stuffed my hands in my pockets. "I may have exaggerated my role in events for dramatic purposes."

The End.

About the Author

Award-winning author Brad Chisholm was born in Canada. He is a graduate of OCA&D and worked in advertising before becoming a writer. He lives in L.A. with his wife, writer and attorney Claire Kim and their son Cole. His previous works, co-authored with Claire Kim, are *K-Town Confidential* and *Kat & Maus*, both published by Black Rose Writing.

Thank you so much for reading one of **Brad Chisholm's** novels.
If you enjoyed our book, please check out our recommendation
for your next great read!

K-Town Confidential by Brad Chisholm and Claire Kim

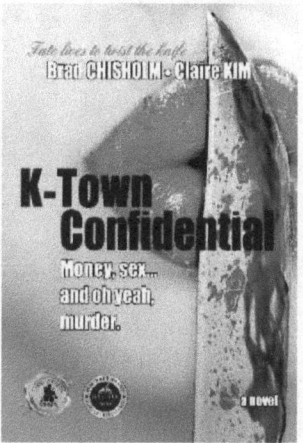

"An enjoyable zigzagging plot, though it's the rather sensational
Holly who leaves the strongest impression." *–KIRKUS REVIEWS*